"Your tea's made and I found the crackers. And I must say that if this is your normal diet—"

"It's not," Jenna said shortly. "It just happens to be brought on by the fact that I'm expecting *your* baby."

"Ah, yes, the baby. That's one of the things I wanted to talk about," Edmund said. "The way I see things, your family and friends are going to have a feeding frenzy over your latest crisis. They'll be merciless in doling out the pity and advice."

"If this is supposed to make me feel better, it's not working. I've already come to the same conclusion, and I'd hardly call it comforting." Jenna replied.

"So head them off at the pass. Show up with a husband."

"In case you hadn't noticed," she said tartly, "they're a vanishing species where I'm concerned. How do you propose I find one?"

"You've already got your man. I'm volunteering for the job."

Back by popular demand...

EXPECTING

She's sexy,
successful...
and
PREGNANT!

Relax and enjoy our fabulous series
about couples whose passion results in
pregnancies...sometimes unexpected! Of course,
the birth of a baby is always a joyful event, and we
can guarantee that our characters will become
besotted moms and dads—but what happened in
those nine months before?

Share the surprises, emotions, drama
and suspense as our parents-to-be come
to terms with the prospect of bringing a
new life into the world. All will discover that
the business of making babies brings with it
the most special love of all....

Our next arrival will be
For the Babies' Sakes
by Sara Wood
Harlequin Presents #2280

Catherine Spencer

THE PREGNANT BRIDE

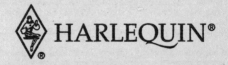

HARLEQUIN®

TORONTO • NEW YORK • LONDON
AMSTERDAM • PARIS • SYDNEY • HAMBURG
STOCKHOLM • ATHENS • TOKYO • MILAN • MADRID
PRAGUE • WARSAW • BUDAPEST • AUCKLAND

ISBN 0-373-12269-1

THE PREGNANT BRIDE

First North American Publication 2002.

Printed in U.S.A.

CHAPTER ONE

EDMUND noticed her the minute she came into the dining room, not because she was beautiful, which she was, but because, in a roomful of people, she was so profoundly alone.

He was alone, too, and wallowing in it. Not so with her. The eyes staring at the menu were blank, the face wiped clean of expression. For some reason he couldn't begin to fathom, she'd shut down inside so completely that if the room had burst into flames, she probably wouldn't have noticed.

Not your concern, buddy, he told himself, gesturing for his bill. *You've got enough problems of your own, without taking on a perfect stranger's.*

Still, he lingered at his table, watching her; noting the absence of rings on her fingers, the formal, upswept hairdo incongruously at odds with her sweater and slacks. When she spoke to the waiter, she cupped her chin in one hand to support her mouth because that was the only way she could control its trembling. Oh yeah, something was definitely wrong!

Her server knew it, too. He didn't make eye contact. Didn't hover obsequiously, reciting the chef's special creations of the day. He wanted away from her quickly, before whatever ailed her infected him, too. Her barely contained misery was an affront. *Romantic ambience* were key words when it came to describing The Inn. Tragic heroines, however lovely, had no place there.

Just briefly she looked up, a glance so wary and fearful that when their gazes locked, Edmund caught himself smiling at her and shrugging conspiratorially. *Hang in there, sweet pea! Don't let him spook you. You've got as much right to be here as anyone.*

She glared back at him and stiffened her already poker-straight spine.

He felt his face crack into a grin he couldn't control. Damn, but he admired her spirit! Faced with personal crises, the women he'd dated over the last couple of year either fled to the therapist's couch or a weekend at one of those fat farms where, for the price of a mere few thousand dollars, their stress and cellulite could be flushed away in one fell swoop.

But not this woman. She was the kind who'd go down fighting—or so he thought, until her drink arrived. Scotch, if he was any judge, and a double, to boot. Confronted by it, she sort of reared back in her seat and regarded the liquor suspiciously. Finally, after debating matters for a full thirty seconds or more, she picked up the glass. Her expression reminded him of a child faced with a dose of foul-tasting but good-for-you medicine, and he pretty well guessed what was coming next.

Willing her to look his way again, he shook his head. *Don't do it, lady! It's not going to solve a thing!*

Whatever mental powers he possessed failed him though, because she clearly didn't get the message. Raising the glass, she tossed back half the contents in a single gulp.

Clearly, from the way she gagged and choked, she and whiskey weren't on familiar terms, and the effect was immediate, devastating and irreparable. The heat of the liquor burning down her throat chewed away the icy calm in which she'd encased herself, and what started as a booze-induced sting to her eyes rapidly dissolved into silent, body-wrenching sobs.

She gulped, dipped her head to try to hide her face, struggled to draw a breath. But once started, there was no stopping the flood and the tears kept coming. Caught in the rays of the westerly sun, they splashed off the end of her nose and dribbled down her sweater like crystal beads come unstrung.

Well, hell! Hard-boiled where women and their sob sessions were concerned he might have become, but he couldn't just sit there and watch her fall apart, especially since no one else was going to help her and she was beyond being able to help herself. "Put the lady's drink on my bill," he directed the waiter and, shoving back his chair, waded in to slay whatever dragons were tormenting her.

She was making a public spectacle of herself! Of all the hurt and embarrassment she'd suffered that day, the fact that she couldn't control the hideous sobs gurgling and sputtering out of her mouth was the ultimate indignity. That morning, someone else was accountable for having humiliated her; now she was the perpetrator and had no one to blame but herself.

Knowing that and being able to do something about it, though, were two different things. Try as she might to control them, the sobs choked out and echoed around the room, a socially obscene gaffe which no one could have missed. Although too polite to stare openly, everybody was sneaking a look, from the teenage busboy in the corner, to the man seated two tables away, the one who, just minutes before, had tried to pick her up with his sly smile and the practiced shrug of his no doubt impressive shoulders.

Lounge lizard! If it weren't that she was openly slobbering into her napkin, a sight surely guaranteed to put off even the most determined skirt-chaser, he'd no doubt have made his next move by now and offered to buy her a drink, followed by the suggestion that they go somewhere private to admire the sunset.

And part of you would have welcomed the suggestion, an

obnoxious little voice inside her head sneered. *Any man sparing you a second glance not dripping with pity is preferable to this morning's unmitigated rejection.*

But there was a limit to what even he was prepared to tolerate. From the corner of her eye, Jenna saw him mutter something to the waiter, then head straight past her, anxious to escape before she made an even worse exhibition of herself. And because she was a fool, too steeped in self-pity to care about the impression she was creating, her tears flowed even faster.

Then, shockingly, a hand—warm, firm and unmistakably masculine—touched her shoulder, slid down her spine almost to her waist, and urged her to her feet. And a voice, deep and resonant with authority, murmured in her ear. "Okay, sweet pea, enough of this. What say we take the rest of the show outside?"

Sweet pea, indeed! She should have been offended at the familiarity, the condescension. If she'd been in her right mind, instead of wallowing in useless self-pity, she'd have told him so in no uncertain terms. But she hadn't been herself since that morning and beggars couldn't be choosers. At that moment he was the only savior she had so, when he offered her his arm, instead of slapping it aside, she grabbed hold as if it were a life belt and let him shepherd her past the stares and the whispers infiltrating the dining room.

Outside, the cool evening air brushed her face and marginally restored her composure. "Thank you," she sniffled, except that it came out sounding more like *"Phn-k!"* because her throat was so waterlogged with tears still.

"Sure," he said, steering her toward a covered flight of steps. "Just hang on till we get to the beach, then you can howl to your heart's content. There'll be no one there to hear but the gulls and they're so busy making their own racket, they won't even notice yours."

She stepped down to a vast stretch of shoreline scoured

clean by the receding tide and deserted except for a couple with two children and a dog, far enough away that they were mere dots on the horizon. Except for the man at her side, Jenna was alone. She could shriek until she was hoarse, but what was the use when, at the end of it all, nothing would have changed?

So instead, she fell into step beside the man as he struck out for the water's edge, grateful that he didn't feel a need to fill the silence between them with empty conversation. Seeming bent on his own thoughts, he adjusted his stride to hers, shoved his hands in his jacket pocket, and fixed his gaze to where the lowering sun painted the tips of the waves gold.

Gradually, the convulsive sobbing eased and she could breathe again—deep, reviving breaths, laced with the clean tang of salt and the sharp bite of an early, west-coast May evening. The constriction which, since morning, had gripped her throat and made swallowing painful, softened. Except for the gritty aftermath of tears inflaming her eyes, she was almost herself again. "Thank you," she said again. "I don't know what I'd have done if you hadn't stepped in when you did."

He nodded. "Glad to help. Feel like talking about whatever's got you tied up in knots?"

"I...no, I don't think so."

"It might help and I'm a pretty good listener."

"I made a mistake, that's all," she said.

He gave a nonchalant shrug. "So you're fallible like the rest of us. Don't go beating yourself up about it."

"A *huge* mistake."

"Most mistakes can be rectified, one way or another."

"Not this one."

He let his glance flicker over her before returning his attention to the sunset. "That bad, huh? What did you do, kill somebody?"

It was the wrong question to ask. "I should have!" she said fiercely. "If I'd had a gun, I *would* have!"

"Uh-oh!"

She glared at him. "What's *that* supposed to mean?"

"When a woman overreacts like that to a purely hypothetical question, it's either because she's got man trouble or she's criminally deranged. If you were the latter, you'd have gone for the waiter with your steak knife. Instead, you tried to put a brave face on things—and you might have succeeded if you'd steered clear of the booze."

"I am not a drinker," she said stiffly. "At least, not as a rule. But tonight…"

"Tonight you needed something to dull the pain."

"Yes."

"So this is about a man?"

"Yes."

"I take it the relationship, such as it was, is over and that he's the one who ended it?"

"Yes." The word exploded on a sigh that seemed to start in the soles of her feet and drag every ounce of energy out of her.

He rocked back on his heels and surveyed her critically. "Even with your face all red and puffy from crying, you're a fine looking woman. Beautiful, in fact. Seems to me you could take your pick of men. What made you latch on to such a bozo?"

Jenna thought of Mark's spaniel brown eyes, as different from this stranger's penetrating blue stare as melting chocolate from ice; of his endearing grin, more reminiscent of a little boy's than a hard-nosed financier's. "I fell in love with him," she quavered.

"A hell of a lot more than he fell in love with you, apparently! If you want my opinion, you're well rid of him."

"I don't want your opinion," she snapped. She'd gone through enough already that day without this…this *creature* pontificating on her situation and handing out Band-Aid solutions when she was *bleeding* inside!

"I thought a bit of down-to-earth common sense might help, but if you'd rather wallow in misery…" He lifted his shoulders in yet another shrug so graphically executed that there was no need for him to finish the sentence.

Suddenly, she saw herself through his eyes, and it wasn't a pretty picture. A weeping, hysterical woman knocking back double scotches and losing control of herself in front of a roomful of people was in no position to take out her misery on the one person who'd shown her compassion. "I was left at the altar," she confessed, the very act of speaking the words aloud leaving her hollow with pain.

"When?"

The sneaking suspicion that she owed her savior something more than the bare bones she'd so far offered overcame her earlier reticence. "This morning."

"Oh, boy!" He whistled through his teeth. "Small wonder you're such a mess."

"Perhaps, but that doesn't entitle me to be rude to you, or to intrude on your time. I'm sure your plans for the evening didn't involve playing nursemaid to a jilted bride." She squared her shoulders and did her best to project the image of a woman in control and well able to stand on her own two feet which, considering her recent bout of weeping, was a lost cause from the outset. "Please don't feel you have to stay out here with me. I'll be perfectly all right by myself," she said, her voice wobbling dangerously.

"Garbage!" he declared flatly. "You've been dumped on what should be the happiest day of your life, and you shouldn't be alone. Surely there's someone who could be here with you—a friend, or a family member?"

"No! I don't want…people to…know where I am."

He stepped back and searched her face incredulously. "Are you saying that after being stood up at the altar and left emotionally distraught, you just disappeared without a word to anyone?''

"That's right." She returned his gaze defiantly.

"What about your relatives and friends? They must be worried out of their minds. Or didn't that strike you as important?''

The censure in his voice stirred her to an unwelcome guilt which, in turn, put her once again on the defensive. "What would you have done in my place? Invite all the guests to the reception and have it turn into a wake with them all commiserating with the forlorn bride?''

He rolled his eyes. "Cripes, do you always go overboard like this? Couldn't you have found a happy medium and shown some consideration for your family's feelings? They're probably beside themselves with concern for you.''

"If you only knew…!'' she began, then clamped her mouth shut and turned away from him because, even if she tried to explain, he'd just think she was trying to milk her situation for more sympathy than he had to spare. And to be fair, how could a stranger be expected to understand the hopes and expectations her family had pinned on her marriage to one of the city's wealthiest financiers?

"We'll finally be accepted where we belong,'' her mother had crowed to her father. "Doors will open, you'll see! We'll be rubbing shoulders with the rich and famous. Mark will give our son a position in the firm, something appropriate for a young man of Glen's ability. And with a few words dropped in the right ear, Amber's career will be made overnight.''

"He's marrying Jenna, not the whole family,'' her father had tried to point out. "Mark doesn't owe the rest of us any favors.''

But her mother had been undeterred. "Why not, when he can so easily afford them?''

Was that what had made Mark change his mind at the last

minute? Had he felt he was nothing more than a cash cow, even though Jenna would have loved him just as dearly if he'd been dirt-poor?

The breeze picked up, tugging at the formal hairdo her stylist had created just that morning. Hugging her arms against the chill, Jenna swung back to the stranger. "I left a note at my parents' house telling them I'd be away for a few days and not to worry about me. Satisfied?"

"I guess," he said, "but I still don't see why you'd want to cut yourself off from them." He inclined his head toward The Inn perched majestically on the rocks to their right. "Or why you'd want to hole up in a place designed for couples and lovers. Seems to me that's just rubbing salt in the wounds."

He subjected her to another penetrating stare and she felt color stealing into her cheeks. "Oh, brother, let me guess!" he exclaimed, enlightenment dawning. "You were supposed to honeymoon here, right?"

"At least I knew I'd have a room reserved," she said defensively. "The bridal suite, in fact, complete with champagne on ice and flowers by the bucketful."

He circled her as if she were some rare species of sea life accidentally washed ashore. "You've got to be kidding!"

She stared at her feet, feeling more foolish by the minute. "At least it's the last place anyone would think to come looking for me."

He laughed then, a rich warm rumble of amusement borne away on the breeze. "You're going to be okay, you know that?" he said, tipping up her chin with his finger and smiling down at her. "Any woman with the guts to face her demons in the one place she'd expected to find true love is a real survivor. What say we head back to The Inn and I buy us both a drink to celebrate?"

Well, why not? The only thing waiting for her in the suite

was a bed big enough for two and no one to share it with. "All right," she said. "Thank you. You're very kind."

"Yeah," he said, tucking her hand under his arm and towing her back the way they'd come. "But keep it under your hat, okay? I don't want the word to get out."

His name was Edmund Delaney and she found herself enjoying his company more than she'd have thought possible an hour before. He was an entertaining host, articulate, amusing, and unquestionably the most attractive man in the room. She sat by the fire and sipped the cognac he ordered and, for a little while, she was able to push the fiasco of her wedding day to the back of her mind. Eventually, though, the evening came to an end.

"I'll walk you to your room," he offered and because she dreaded being alone, she accepted.

Taller than Mark, broader across the shoulders, and more powerfully built, he loped up the stairs with the graceful ease of an athlete at the peak of fitness. "Give me your key," he said, when they arrived at her door, and as she handed it over, she noticed his hands were lean and tanned and capable, and just a little callused as if he worked with tools. Mark had a manicure every week and wouldn't have known one end of a hammer from the other.

"Here you are." Edmund pushed open her door, dropped the keys into her palm and folded her fingers over them.

If he'd said, "Sleep well," she'd probably have managed to end the evening with a modicum of dignity, but his more sensitive "Try to get some sleep," had the tears burning behind her eyes all over again.

Mutely, she looked up at him.

His fingers grazing her cheek were gentle. "I know," he murmured. "It isn't going to be easy."

He left her then and she knew a shocking urge to call him back and beg him not to make her face the night alone. It wasn't that she wanted him to make love to her or anything like that; she just needed the warmth of human contact, the feeling that someone in the world cared—not that a two-thousand-dollar wedding dress had gone to waste, or that four hundred guests had been cheated of a seven-course dinner, but that *she* somehow survive the crushing blow to her self-esteem and live to face another day.

Not until his footsteps had faded into silence did she venture into the room. A fire burned in the hearth and beyond the wide windows a half-moon floated over the ocean. The maid had turned down the bed on both sides and left foil-wrapped chocolates on each pillow. Hadn't she noticed there was only one set of luggage, only one toothbrush in the bathroom?

Unable to face the bed, Jenna sank down on the rug before the fire and because there was no longer any ignoring them, let the ghastly events of the day wash over her.

It had begun well enough, with sunshine and clear skies. There'd been no hint of impending disaster as she'd ridden with her father to the church, no sense of something amiss as her bridesmaids fussed with her veil and whispered that the groom and his family had not yet arrived. Mark and his father were often late, held up by international phone calls and such. "That's the price of doing business," Mark had said, when she'd once had the temerity to complain. "Money before pleasure any day of the week."

Including their wedding day, it had seemed!

"They've taken a wrong turn and got lost," her father joked. "Or been stopped for speeding."

But as the minutes stretched and still no groom, the smiles had shrunk and the speculation had begun, rippling over the congregation like wind over a cornfield. Finally, "I have another wedding in half an hour," the minister had said, coming out to where she waited in her wedding finery. "I'm afraid that unless Mr. Armstrong and his party arrive in the next few minutes, we'll have to reschedule your ceremony for another time.''

By then, though, a dull certainty had taken hold and Jenna knew that Mark wasn't going to arrive, not in the next few minutes and not ever. Instead, Paul King, his best man, had shown up, red-faced and apologetic.

''So sorry, Jenna,'' he'd stammered, handing her an envelope. ''Wish I didn't have to be the one to bring you this. Wish there could have been a happier ending....''

The letter was brief and full of empty excuses aimed at softening the blow of rejection. *...afraid I won't make you happy...can't give you what you want...you deserve better, dear Jenna...a wonderful woman who'll make some lucky man a wonderful wife...forgive me...some day you'll thank me...this hurts me as much as I know it will hurt you....*

''What does it say?'' her mother had asked in a horrified whisper, and when she hadn't replied, had snatched the paper out of Jenna's hand, read it for herself, and let out a squawk of outrage. ''He can't do this!'' she'd cried. ''We've got sixty pounds of smoked salmon waiting at the club! Your father had to extend his line of credit at the bank to finance this wedding!''

The bad news had spread quickly, rolling through the church like an anthem. Heads had turned, necks craned, feet shuffled. And throughout it all, Jenna had stood at the door, bouquet dangling from one limp hand, wedding veil floating in the May breeze, silk gown whispering around her ankles and a great empty hole where her heart had been.

What was the correct protocol for a bride left waiting at the altar? Throwing herself off the nearest bridge hadn't appealed although, when she first read the letter, she had, briefly, wished the floor would open up and swallow her. But what her mother referred to as her ''infernal pride'' had come to her rescue. Somehow, from somewhere, she'd manufactured a kind of frozen calm to get herself through the ordeal suddenly confronting her.

Hooking her train over her arm, she made her way back to where the limousines waited and climbed into the one which had brought her to the church and had her honeymoon luggage stowed in the trunk. "There will be no wedding," she informed the startled driver as he raced to close the door for her, and directed him to her apartment.

While he transferred her suitcases to her car, she'd changed into the first clothes she laid hands on, scribbled a note for her parents and given it to him to deliver, and within twenty minutes was speeding down the highway to the ferry terminal. What was supposed to have been the happiest day of her life had turned into a nightmare of titan proportion, witnessed by half the social elite in the province and another hundred from out of town, and she had known only that she had to escape, quickly, before the blessed numbness passed and the pain took hold.

She'd managed pretty well—or so she'd thought. Bolstered by a confidence which in reality was nothing more than a continuation of the daze which had steered her through the hours since her aborted wedding, she'd ignored the voice of caution and decided to brave The Inn's dining room. Why should she hide away in her suite? She'd done nothing to be ashamed of!

But confronting the other diners had proved more of an ordeal than she'd expected. If she'd worn a sign plastered to her forehead, declaring her Abandoned Bride of the Year, she couldn't have felt more exposed or vulnerable.

She owed Edmund Delaney a huge debt of gratitude....

As if they had a will of their own, her eyes swung from their contemplation of the flames in the hearth to the telephone on the little occasional table beside the fireplace.

Should she call him? Invite him to lunch, perhaps, as

thanks for his having saved her from making an even bigger fool of herself at dinner?

Not a smart move, Jenna, her cautious conscience scolded. *Chasing after a man you hardly know, only hours after you were jilted by the man you planned to marry, smacks more of desperation to find a replacement than gratitude!*

True enough! So why was she lifting the receiver, why requesting that a call be put through to the room of one Edmund Delaney? And why, having gone that far, did she stare in horrified fascination at the telephone when he picked up on the second ring, then immediately hang up and flee to the bathroom as if he were in hot pursuit?

There was a phone in there, too. It rang before she had the door closed. "We must have been cut off," Edmund Delaney said, when she finally found the courage to answer. "Good thing it was an in-house call and the front desk was able to reconnect us. What can I do for you?"

CHAPTER TWO

"…UM…" SHE muttered. "Er…who is this? That is, I…um…"

Duplicity didn't come naturally to her and he clearly recognized an amateur when he heard one. Cutting short her bumbling reply, he said curtly, "It's Edmund Delaney, Jenna. And you just phoned me, right?"

"Yes," she admitted faintly, wishing for the second time in a day that seemed doomed never to end, that she could disappear off the face of the earth and spare everyone further grief. "I wanted to make sure I'd…thanked you. Properly, that is. For coming to my rescue at dinner."

He sounded as if he might be having a hard time choking back a laugh when he replied, and she could scarcely blame him. Her pitiful attempt at subterfuge was as transparent as glass. "You thanked me," he said. "And you were very proper."

"But just saying the words doesn't seem enough. I feel you deserve more than that."

Dear heaven, woman, rephrase that quickly before he decides you're making a play for him and offering more than you're prepared to give!

"Wh…what I mean is, may I buy you breakfast in the morning? As a token of my gratitude, you understand? Say about nine, in the main dining room?"

"Afraid not," he said cheerfully. "I won't be here."

Either it was just one rejection too many, or else she was courting insanity to be so crushed by his answer. Clearing her throat to dislodge the great lump of disappointment

19

threatening to strangle her, she aimed for nonchalance. "Oh, that's too bad. Then I guess we won't see each other again."

"I've chartered a boat to take me fishing at dawn and don't expect to be back much before noon."

The rush of relief she experienced at that piece of news was almost as disconcerting as hearing herself suggest, with an eagerness which could only be described as pathetic, "What about lunch, then?"

"I have a better idea," he said, after a small, contemplative pause. "Why don't you come fishing with me? There's nothing like reeling in a fighting salmon to take your mind off your other troubles."

He was being kind. Again. "Thanks, but I think I'll pass. I don't know the first thing about fishing."

"Only one way to learn," he said. "I'll be leaving here about five-thirty. Meet me in the lobby downstairs if you change your mind."

Well, it was out of the question. For a start, all she'd brought with her was her honeymoon luggage and it didn't include hip waders and oilskins, or whatever it was that fishing persons wore. Furthermore, she'd be lousy company and he'd already put up with enough of that. He didn't need the aggravation of wondering if the weepy woman hanging over the side of the boat was planning to end it all by diving headfirst into the saltchuck.

But when, after a night of fitful sleep, she found herself wide-awake at five the next morning, with the beginning of another beautiful day hovering on the horizon, watching the sunrise with Edmund Delaney didn't seem such a bad idea after all.

Because she and Mark had planned to walk on the beach, she *did* have a pair of jeans in her suitcase, and a lightweight jacket and a pair of rubber-soled shoes. The day stretched before her, depressingly empty. And there was nothing more enervating or unattractive than a woman so steeped in self-pity that even *she* was getting tired of herself. So why not take Edmund up on his offer?

She found him leaning against the front desk, thumbing through a map of the area. Dressed in jeans also, with a heavy cream sweater over a navy turtleneck and his dark hair still damp from the shower, he was an undeniably handsome sight. But it was his aura of confidence and strength that brought to her mind the shocking thought that *he'd* never take the easy way out by appointing someone else to do his dirty work, the way Mark had.

Edmund Delaney was made of sterner stuff.

"Well, what do you know!" he said, his smile touching the cold recesses of her heart with surprising warmth. "Looks as if I'm going to have company, after all."

He drove a dark green Lincoln Navigator, a big and powerful vehicle to match the man who owned it. It smelled of leather and a pleasant hint of the Douglas firs which grew in such profusion along the coast.

Settling himself behind the wheel, Edmund fired up the engine and slewed a glance her way. "Ready to catch some fish?"

"Willing to try, at any rate."

His grin was startlingly white in the faint glow of early morning. "Good woman!"

Mark favored a Porsche so sleek and low-slung that, most of the time, the view from the windshield was largely blocked by the rear end of the car in front. In Edmund's vehicle, she was perched up high enough that, if there'd been any other traffic on the road at that hour, she'd have been able to see clear over it to the fishing village nestled at the foot of a steep hill three miles away.

Except for those times when he tuned in to a news station to keep track of the stock market, Mark preferred to listen to classical music. Edmund plugged in a *Best Of Rock 'n' Roll* CD and throughout the journey, thumped the rim of the steering wheel in time to the manic din of Jerry Lee Lewis belting out "Great Balls of Fire."

She was out of her element. She was with a man who could be a serial rapist for all she knew about him. She was planning to spend the day at sea with him. No one knew where she was. No one would miss her—at least not for at least a week, by which time she could be fish food. Her situation had all the makings of a TV murder mystery.

At the very least, she should have been nervous. Instead, she felt safe and warm. Removed from the familiar world and the cares it had thrust at her.

She knew the reprieve was temporary, that ultimately, she'd have to go back and start to put her life together again. But for now, being able to focus on something new and different was enough to let the healing of old wounds begin. And that, surely, was a gift she couldn't afford to turn down.

By the time the Navigator rolled to a stop on the fishing dock, the sky had lightened to a pale aquamarine which reflected coldly off the quiet waters of the harbor. Slinging a canvas bag over one shoulder, Edmund took Jenna's hand and guided her down the ramp toward a fleet of boats bobbing gently on the tide.

"The twenty-four-foot Bayliner on the end is ours and it comes complete with breakfast. If we hustle, we could be out on open water in time to see the sun come up over the mountains."

Not in her wildest dreams had she expected she'd truly enjoy herself. She'd viewed the excursion as just another way to distract herself from dwelling on the shambles of her wedding day. But the peace and beauty of the setting worked an amazing magic.

Although the air was chilly, the sky was blue, the waves a gentle rolling motion beneath the boat, and the coffee and freshly baked sweet rolls which Hank the skipper served for breakfast, pure heaven.

"You doing okay?" Edmund asked, as they motored out to a point about five miles north of the village. "Not feeling queasy or anything?"

She shook her head. "I'm more relaxed than I've been in weeks. The days leading up to the wedding were hectic, what with the various parties and showers." Cradling her coffee mug in her hands, she leaned against the bulkhead, closed her eyes, and lifted her face to the sun. "In fact, I'm so comfortable I could easily fall asleep."

She hadn't intended acting on the words, especially not so promptly, but when she next became aware of her surroundings, the boat rocked at anchor, her head was cushioned by a life jacket, a blanket covered her from the waist down, the sun was riding high above the mountains, her watch showed a quarter to nine—and she needed a washroom in the worst way.

Above her on a sort of raised deck, the men were chatting idly. Hank sat in a swivel chair which allowed him to keep an eye on the fishing poles angled in brackets attached to either side of the back of the boat. Edmund lounged against the instrument panel. Trying to be inconspicuous, Jenna slithered off the bench and down the laddered steps to the cabin, trailing the blanket behind her.

Below, she found a table flanked by two upholstered benches, a sloping desk covered with navigation charts, a kitchen of sorts—and, praise the Lord, a washroom! Heaving a sigh of relief, she made a beeline for the latter.

She returned on deck to a scene of high excitement. Edmund hauled on one of the lines while Hank hung over the side of the boat with a net in his hand, all the while bellowing, "Keep the tip up! Keep reeling him in!"

She saw a flash of silver a few yards off, a thrashing just below the surface of the water, and shortly after, Hank scooped a salmon into the net and brought it on board.

Jumping down to where she stood, Edmund seized her

around the waist and practically hoisted her off her feet. "Would you look at that beauty!" he gloated. "A coho, and sixteen pounds at least!"

Personally, the closest she ever came to any kind of salmon was after it had been nicely filleted, perfectly grilled, and served on a plate with a lemon and parsley garnish. Although she found it delicious, it certainly never stirred her to the kind of exuberant delight infecting Edmund. But she hadn't the heart to tell him so. Staggering a little as he released her, she said instead, "You're right, it's beautiful! Now what do you do with it?"

"Club it over the head and put it out of its misery," Hank informed her laconically. She must have blanched at the image he brought to mind, because he went on, "Might be best if you went back below deck and scrambled up a dozen eggs while we take care of business."

Edmund nodded agreement. "Go," he said. "You don't need to see this and it's been a long time since we had fresh coffee. You know how to use a propane stove, or do you want me to light it for you?"

"I can manage," she said, unable to drag her gaze away from the fish still flopping around on the deck, and mortified to find her eyes suddenly filling with tears. Poor thing! Just moments before it had been wild and free; now it had to die to satisfy the primeval hunting instincts in a couple of otherwise civilized men.

Noticing her distress, Edmund said quietly, "You want me to toss it back overboard, sweet pea?"

"No," she said, dashing away the tears. "From the looks of it, it would probably die anyway."

"I'm afraid you're right."

"You must think I'm an absolute fool to get so overwrought about a mere fish."

His blue eyes darkened and his voice was almost tender when he replied, "I don't think any such thing. Go crack some eggs in a bowl and find a frying pan. And if you need help with the stove, just give a shout.''

She found butter, eggs and mushrooms in the cooler, more rolls in a bag on the tiny counter, coffee in a jar by the sink, and a cast iron frying pan in the oven.

When Edmund swung down into the cabin fifteen minutes later, she'd buttered half a dozen rolls and had a huge mushroom omelet sizzling in the pan.

''Came to lend a hand,'' he said, ''but I can see I'm not needed.''

''Not in the kitchen, at least.''

He ducked his head until his eyes were on a level with hers. ''On a boat, it's called a galley, Jenna.''

Kitchen, galley—call it what he liked, it wasn't designed for two, especially not when one of the occupants stood over six feet and weighed close to a hundred and ninety pounds. No matter how careful she was, every time she moved, whether it was to turn the omelet or pour boiling water over the coffee grounds, one part of her or another brushed against him.

She could detect the faint smell of soap on his skin, feel the warmth of his breath in her hair, the heat of his body at her back. The experience left her oddly short of breath.

''You want to eat outside?'' she practically wheezed.

''You bet. Got to keep an eye out to make sure the fishing lines stay clear.''

She stuffed the rolls into a basket, plunked three coffee mugs on top and shoved the lot into his hands. ''Then make yourself useful and take all this on deck while I finish the eggs.''

''Sure. And don't even think about trying to climb into the cockpit with that coffeepot. I'll bring it up.''

I pay other people to take care of things like that, Mark had informed her, the one time she'd made the mistake of asking him to help clear away the dishes after she'd made dinner for him at her apartment. *Once we're married, you won't have to lift a finger. We'll have an entire staff to look after the cooking and housekeeping.*

But I like cooking, she'd protested. *And I like being in charge of my own kitchen.*

There's a difference between being in charge and taking on the role of household drudge. Armstrong wives don't appear in public with dishpan hands.

Lithe and agile, Edmund swung down into the cabin and closed in on her again. "How much longer before those eggs are ready, woman?" he said, eyeing the frying pan devoutly. "The smells floating up top have driven us to drink. Hank's lacing the coffee with rum."

"They're done," she said, dividing the omelet into three unequal parts and sliding the two larger portions onto plates. "These are for you and Hank and I'll be right behind you with mine."

When he'd gone, she fanned her face with a dish towel and decided there was a lot of truth to the old saying about getting out of the kitchen if a person couldn't take the heat. She definitely couldn't take the kind of heat Edmund Delaney generated!

His head reappeared in the open hatch. "Want me to bring up anything else?"

What she wanted was a few minutes in which to collect herself, because try as she might, she found herself constantly comparing him to Mark and finding her former fiancé coming up short. How could that be when Mark was the man she wanted to spend the rest of her life with? The possible answers were too disturbing to contemplate.

"Good grub," Hank announced, when she came up on deck. "You ever want a job, you've got one. Tourist season's just around the corner and I could use a cook like you."

The idea had merit. Her bruised spirit craved the prospect

of a simple life, uncomplicated by the demands of a family who, sadly, had viewed her marriage to Mark as a passport to high society and easy living. The anonymity of being a stranger in a remote village cut off from the stress and bustle of the Lower Mainland held enormous appeal.

Edmund was watching her closely. "Tempted by the idea?"

"Good grief!" she said, pressing her palms to her cheeks. "Am I that easy to read?"

"Clear as glass," he said, his blue eyes disconcertingly intent. "Your face is an open book. You'd make a lousy poker player."

I make a lousy everything, she almost replied, the self-pity she'd managed to subdue suddenly rearing up again.

Was it the bright, sunny day that made her fight it? The grandeur of the scene around her beside which her little tragedy seemed pitifully insignificant? Or the man sitting across from her and seeing into her heart so much more clearly than Mark ever had? "Then I'd better stick to cooking," she said, drumming up a smile even though the effort made her face ache.

Hank looked hopeful. "You takin' me up on my offer?"

"Thanks, but no," she said, her smile more genuine this time. "I have other things I need to do."

Like fighting her demons, laying certain ghosts to rest, and facing the rest of her life without Mark.

She gave an involuntary shudder at the enormity of the task facing her, and hugged her elbows close to her chest.

"Wind's pickin' up," Hank observed, squinting at her in the sunlight. "Usually does about this time of day. Might be best if you found something a bit heavier to wear than that flimsy jacket you brought with you."

"I don't need—" she began, but Edmund cut her off.

"Yes, you do." He reached into his canvas bag and pulled

out an extra sweater. "Put this on, sweet pea. It'll cut the wind out and keep you from catching cold."

It was easier not to argue, and truth to tell, comforting to have him care. Obediently, she slipped the sweater over head. Thick and heavy like the one he was wearing, its sleeves hung well below the tips of her fingers and the hem reached almost to her knees.

"Sure it's big enough?" Hank snickered. "Looks to me as if there's room for two in there."

"Not quite," she said, her senses swimming as Edmund slid his fingers along the back of her neck to free her hair trapped inside the collar. "But you're right. I won't make any Best Dressed Lists with it."

"It isn't the packaging that counts," he said, slinging a arm around her shoulders and giving her a friendly hug. "I thought you were smart enough to know that."

He meant nothing special by the gesture, she was sure. But that didn't stop her from wanting to lean into his solid strength, and pretend, just for a minute, that she *was* on her honeymoon and married to a man like him.

Heavenly days, where was her head, that she'd even entertain such an idea?

"Is it too late for me to try my hand at fishing?" she said, hurriedly pulling away and pretending an interest in the contents of the tackle box before she showed herself completely lacking in good judgment and wrapped her arms around him.

"Sure you want to try?"

She inspected the wicked-looking hooks and grimaced. "Not if I have to use one of these. They're instruments of torture."

"You can use a barbless hook," Hank said. "Lots of folks do if they can't stand the sight of blood."

She ventured a glance at Edmund. "I suppose you think I'm ridiculously squeamish."

"You suppose wrong—again. We've already got one salmon in the cooler. We don't need another."

"Well," she said doubtfully, "if you're sure you don't mind...?"

"I'll make you a deal. You can throw back anything you catch if you'll come with me to The Dungeness Trap tonight."

"Dungeness Trap?"

"Don't look so suspicious. It's a restaurant in town that serves the best crab you've ever tasted, not the local den of iniquity!"

"I don't know...."

"I'm not asking you to sign over your firstborn, Jenna," he said persuasively. "I'm simply inviting you to have dinner with me."

"But I can't keep imposing on your time like this. You've already done so much and been so...kind."

"Hey, I'm no Boy Scout, if that's what you're thinking! The way I have it figured, you owe me. I've had to listen to your tale of woe and it's your turn to listen to the grisly details of mine." He extended his palm. "So what do you say? Do we have a deal?"

She placed her hand in his and tried to dismiss as indigestion the little spurt of pleasure churning her stomach as his fingers closed around hers. "We have a deal."

"Sweet pea," he said, his grin so disarming that she went slightly weak at the knees, "you just made my day!"

From the outside, the restaurant looked like little more than a dimly lit shack perched on pilings over the water. Inside, though, it was cosy and comfortable, with oil lamps on the tables, heat blasting from the big open hearth, and fishing nets strung with glass floats anchored from the ceiling. A wine rack covered one wall. At the rear of the room, a woman played a guitar. Beyond a serving hatch was the kitchen with a brick bread oven and huge stainless steel pots simmering on a gleaming range.

"Just as well I made a reservation," Edmund said, after they'd been shown to a table overlooking the harbor. "The place is packed."

None of the men wore ties, though, and for the most part, the women were in slacks and sweaters. "I'm afraid I'm very much overdressed," Jenna said, nervously smoothing the full skirt of her velvet dinner dress.

Edmund looked up from the wine list he'd been perusing and frowned. "Didn't you hear me, this morning? It's what's underneath the surface that matters."

"Mark felt appearances were critically important."

"Mark sounds like an ass."

Determined to be fair, she said, "No. It's just that his family is well-known and he has a reputation to uphold. He was brought up to believe that since he's handling other people's money, it's important to project the right image. Clients like to feel they're in capable hands."

"And you bought that load of rubbish?"

She looked away, embarrassed. What would he say if she admitted that, after they became engaged, Mark had gradually taken over picking out her wardrobe for her, right down to the shade of her stockings? *As an Armstrong wife, you'll be scrutinized from head to toe every time you appear in public. Slip up and your photo will be plastered all over tomorrow's newspapers.*

"Hey, I'm sorry!" Edmund reached across and covered her hand with his. "You've got enough to deal with, without me getting on your case. I've never met the guy and have no business passing judgment on him. But just for the record, what you're wearing now is stunning. Blue suits you."

"It's part of my trousseau. The only clothes I brought with me were those I'd packed for my honeymoon."

He leaned back and gave her such a thorough inspection that she practically squirmed. "Mark doesn't know what he's missing, Jenna. If he did, he'd surely be here now, instead of me.''

''Oh, no!'' she exclaimed, more rattled by his compliment than she cared to admit. ''This isn't his kind of place at all!'' Then, realizing what she'd said, she clapped a horrified hand to her mouth.

''Too upscale, you mean?'' Edmund's eyes danced with mischief.

''Oh!'' she gasped. ''You must think me *so* ungracious!''

His face took on a sober cast and he rearranged his cutlery before finally saying, ''Can I ask you a question?''

''Of course.''

''What was it about this Mark person that made you decide to marry him?''

She lifted her shoulders, mystified that he couldn't figure that out for himself. ''I loved him.''

''Why?''

''I don't understand what you mean. Love doesn't have to have a reason.''

''Sure it does, Jenna. We might like a lot of people, but as a rule, we love very few. What made him special?''

She thought about that for a minute, then said, ''At first, he was interesting and fun and exciting...and...''

And a little bit insecure. Too much under his father's controlling thumb. Too much in thrall to the family name and reputation.

''Go on.''

''He seemed to need me.'' *I made him feel important in his own right. With me, he was somebody other than the son who always did his father's bidding.* ''We became friends.''

''And lovers?''

''Eventually, yes.'' Silly to feel uncomfortable with the admission. She was twenty-seven, after all; well past the age of consent. ''We were compatible. Comfortable with each other. His family accepted us as a couple. So, when he proposed...''

I couldn't think of a good reason to say no.

"...I accepted. I was ready for marriage and I thought we'd be happy together." Irritated to find herself trying to justify a decision which, at the time, had seemed absolutely right, she flung out her hands. "What does it matter? He obviously didn't agree, and now I have to accept that, too."

"How did he break the news that the marriage was off?"

"He had his best man deliver a letter to the church."

"He had his best man deliver a letter?" Edmund made no effort to mask his disgust. "Jeez, I take back my apology. The guy's pure pond scum!"

"He's not nearly as bad as I've made him sound. If anything, he's a rather unhappy man. I thought I could change that. Apparently, I was wrong."

"A guy who sends someone else to do his dirty work isn't fit to be called a man, Jenna! And what I find hard to understand is why you feel compelled to go on defending him."

"Because if I don't," she cried, at her wits' end with his probing questions, "I look like an even bigger fool for having agreed to marry him in the first place. And my pride's taken enough of a beating for one week."

Edmund drew in a long breath and gestured for the waiter. "Mark's the fool, sweet pea," he said, "but if you can't see that without my having to beat you over the head with the idea, we might as well drop the subject."

They feasted on steamed crab dipped in melted butter and washed down with white wine, but although the meal was every bit as delicious as he'd promised, Edmund became increasingly withdrawn and never did make good on his promise to share some of his own history. Nor did he suggest lingering once they'd finished eating. Indeed, his taciturnity during the drive back to The Inn made her wonder if he regretted having invited her to dinner to begin with.

The path from the parking area to The Inn wove among plantings of shrubbery interspersed with the pale faces of daffodils. Concealed floodlights showcased the mighty cedars looming in the background. Strategically placed benches just big enough for two lurked in the shadows. Piano music drifted through the darkness, the notes falling soft and clear in the night.

Everything about the place spelled couples, romance, honeymoons, happy-ever-after. Added to Edmund's aloof silence, it was more than she could bear.

Just a few yards farther on, the path forked, with one way leading directly to The Inn's front door and the other descending to the beach. As they approached it, Edmund stopped. "I'm too restless to turn in, so I'm going for a walk," he said, looking pointedly at her high heels. "I'd ask you to join me but you'd break an ankle in those shoes, so I'll say good night instead. You should sleep well after the day you've had."

Numbly, she watched him turn away, and willed herself to do the same. To walk into The Inn and not look back. To accept that her interlude with him had come to its inevitable end.

His silhouette became indistinct, swallowed up by the night. The sound of his footsteps crunching over the gravel grew fainter.

Do him and yourself a favor and disappear inside before you say something you'll live to regret, Jenna! He can't fix what's broken in your life and you have no business expecting him to try. He's already done enough.

She swallowed, and braced herself to face the night alone. Her self-confidence had already eroded into near oblivion. Why expose it to further abuse? But no amount of common sense could ease the raging loneliness in her heart, or prevent her from calling out just before he disappeared from sight, "Edmund, wait! Don't go without me, please!"

CHAPTER THREE

HE THOUGHT he'd done it—removed himself, permanently, from a situation grown too complex, too fast—but the naked pain in her voice caught up with him just before he moved out of earshot and much though he'd have liked to, he couldn't walk away from it.

Burying a sigh, he waited as she stumbled over the coarse gravel toward him. A gentleman would probably have rushed forward to steady her before she broke her neck in her flimsy little shoes, but he'd never aspired to be anything other than what he was: a working guy who'd made a pile of money by learning from experience never to make the same mistake twice.

A fat lot of good that rule of thumb was doing him now, though. Knowing he'd always been a sucker for a bird with a broken wing should have been reason enough for him to steer clear of her in the first place. That he'd persisted in ignoring the warning bells clanging loud and clear in his mind and had chosen instead to protract the association, was nothing short of foolhardy.

"What?" Frustration, as much with himself as her, had him barking the question at her.

If only she'd taken umbrage or flight at his brusque tone! But she was too wounded, too crushed in spirit. "I can't…face going up to that empty room," she said wretchedly, flinging herself at him.

Good idea or nor, his arms closed around her. She was so slight, so fragile, that to shove her away was unthinkable. But to let her remain pressed close against him like that…!

34

Jeez, it was all the encouragement needed for certain parts due south of his brain to rise to action.

"Listen, Jenna," he said, sounding as if he'd just choked on ground glass, "this isn't such a good idea. I know you're going through a bad time right now, but it'd be better if you were to turn to the people who care about you."

"No," she said, clinging to him and lifting her face to his so that, even though he'd thought it was black as Hades under the trees, enough light filtered through from the gardens for him to see the tears glimmering in her huge dark eyes, and feel himself drowning in them. "I don't need them. I need *you!*"

"How can you need someone you don't even know?"

"For precisely that reason! When you look at me, you don't see a pathetic bride without a groom, or a daughter who's made a laughing stock of her family. You see *me*— an ordinary woman, just like any other."

Ordinary, my hind foot! She was a lovely, sensitive, tenderhearted creature who felt other people's pain as deeply as her own. A woman in desperate need of the kind of loving which would restore her faith in herself—the kind of loving his brain told him she'd do better to seek elsewhere, but which his less cerebral components clamored to accommodate. Another good reason to put an end to things before they grew even more seriously out of hand!

"I can't give you what you're looking for, sweet pea," he said hoarsely. "I come with too much excess baggage of my own."

Briefly, she sagged against him as if all the fight and courage had been blasted out of her. Then, with a flash of the courage which had drawn him to her from the first, she pushed herself away from him. "Of course you can't," she whispered, her voice tinted with shame and her body—every slender, desirable inch of it—poised for escape. "Whatever possessed me to suggest that you could?"

For the second time in as many minutes, he had the chance to cut and run out of her life as easily as he'd blundered into it. So what the devil prompted him to haul her back into his arms, and stroke the soft, dark hair away from her face? What sort of masochist was he to search out her mouth and kiss her as if she was the last woman on earth and there was no tomorrow?

The insatiable kind, that's what, and she'd have done them both a favor if she'd smacked him across the head for his nerve. Maybe that would have spared them both a lot of grief. Instead, her mouth softened beneath his and she sank against him in total surrender.

To his credit, he tried to put a halt to the situation. But when he went to break the kiss, her little whimper of distress scored a direct hit to...

What? His heart? Impossible! He was thirty-five, for Pete's sake, not fifteen, and knew better than to buy that kind of codswallop on the strength of a twenty-four-hour acquaintance with a pretty woman. His conscience? Hell, it was nothing more than a dying whisper desperately trying to make itself heard over the caterwauling of rampant lust! Good deed for the day? Fat chance! He'd been telling her the truth when he said he was no Boy Scout.

"I shouldn't have done that," he muttered, dragging his lips away from hers before he made things even more dangerously volatile by bringing his tongue into play. "It was a very bad idea."

She didn't argue, at least not in so many words. She just brought her soft, smooth little hand up to his cheek and touched him as wonderingly as if she'd just discovered her own personal guardian angel.

"Jenna," he croaked, afraid that the distant thunder echoing in his blood boded no good for either of them, "you're pushing your luck."

She slid both arms around his waist and leaned her head

on his chest. "My luck," she said dreamily, "hit rock bottom yesterday. But thanks to you, it's starting to improve."

If his survival instincts weren't all tangled up in hunger for something he had no right wanting, he'd march her back to The Inn, pack her off to bed by *herself,* in her own room, then hightail it out of her life before he compounded his already manifest sins.

If he possessed one ounce of decency, he wouldn't be tracing a path from her chin to her throat and fantasizing about how she'd look without any clothes on.

If he had a grain of self-respect, he'd back away from her instead of letting her know he was primed for seduction in the most obvious way a man could convey such a message to a woman.

And if the damned Inn weren't so fixated on honeymooners, it wouldn't have made it so easy for a couple to be alone at every turn. There wouldn't be shadowed spotlights pearling the night, or a lullaby of surf whispering ashore, or the scent of cedar and fir and hemlock sweetening the air.

"Maybe," he said, wrestling with vanishing control, "we should figure out what's happening here before we let things go any further."

"Oh, Edmund," she murmured, her hands wreaking havoc over his rib cage, "I'm so tired of trying to look for answers that aren't there. Sometimes, things happen without reason or warning. Just this once, can't we live for the moment and never mind about tomorrow?"

"So what are you suggesting?" He forced the question past a throat gone dry as sandpaper.

"That we follow our feelings, whether or not they make sense."

And just in case he hadn't picked up on what she meant, she tilted her hips against him and lifted her mouth to his again.

He made one last stab at rational argument. "Your feelings are all tied up with another man, Jenna, and I'm not interested in being his stand-in.''

''Nor am I,'' she said, her lips so close that the words brushed his mouth.

Her skin was smooth and warm to his touch. She smelled of flowers, she tasted of innocence, she trembled with need. Her breathing was almost as ragged as his own. He could feel her pulse racing.

''Please make love to me,'' she whimpered, taking his hand and closing it over her breast. ''Please, Edmund, make me feel whole again!''

''Not here,'' he said thickly, urging her back toward The Inn. Whatever else he might be, he wasn't such a lowlife that he'd risk their being discovered by other guests. If they were going to make love—and he knew that, barring some cataclysmic natural disaster, nothing would stop them now— it would be in private. Not in her room but in his. Removed from anything that might remind her of the man whose place he was taking.

The lobby lay deserted, the elevator doors stood open. Pulling her after him into the empty car, he pressed the third-floor button. The doors had barely glided closed before he was searching for her mouth again, the fever to discover her more intimately roaring at fever pitch now that it had been given free rein.

She melted against him, opened her lips to him, clenched her fingers in his hair as his tongue probed the depths of her mouth. So moist, so sweet. So like that other part of her which taunted him with urgent little pelvic thrusts.

She was driving him crazy! How else to justify the insane urge to hit the Stop button and take her, right there on the elevator floor? How otherwise to contain the aching fullness testing his control beyond anything a mere man should have to withstand?

The doors whispered open with a melodious *ding!* ''Talk

about saved by the bell,'' he panted, fairly racing her down the hall.

Moonlight left the corners of his room dark, and swathed the bed in drifts of purple shadow. Her skin took on the luster of pale silk, her hair the sheen of dark satin. He framed her face in his hands and bent his mouth again to hers, hoping to imbue his seduction with at least a little finesse.

But the feel of her, the touch of her, defeated him at the outset. Driven by unwise hunger, he tugged at her clothing, flinging aside one item after another until, at last, he could feast his gaze on her breasts, cup their slender fullness in his hands and take their dusk-tinted peaks in his mouth.

She sagged, as if he were drawing the last ounce of strength from her. Uttered his name on a long, despairing breath. A tremor raced through her.

The same frenzied urgency that possessed him was tearing at her, too, stripping her more naked than he ever could, and reducing her dignity to ashes. They were clawing at each other, their hands delineating every curve, every angle. He heard the soft hiss of ripping fabric. His shirt? Her panties? Egyptian cotton, fine French lace?

It didn't matter. Nothing was more immediate than that they cleave to one another, skin to skin, heartbeat to heartbeat. Nothing, that was, except the primeval tide which had stalked him from the moment he'd kissed her and which, patience at last outrun, refused to hold back a moment longer.

Groaning in defeat, he tumbled her to the floor and buried himself inside her mere milliseconds before the first shattering waves depleted him.

She lay beneath him, her mouth trembling, her eyes wide pools of disappointment.

He bent his forehead to hers and whispered, ''Sweetheart, I'm sorry!''

She touched a finger to his face, traced the outline of his upper lip. "It's all right."

"No," he said, rolling free and drawing her to her feet. "It's all wrong."

He took her hand and led her to the bathroom. Turned on the shower and when the water ran hot, pulled her under the spray with him. He soaped her long, lovely spine, her arms, her legs, until the tension seeped out of her, and her eyes took on a dreamy, unfocused gaze.

Lips slightly apart, she reached for the soap. Her hands roamed over him, lathering the length of his torso in slow, erotic strokes.

Quickly, before she brought him to the brink of destruction a second time, he imprisoned her hands in his and growled, "Uh-uh, Jenna! Cut it out!"

"We aren't going to make love again?" she asked him dazedly.

A firm believer in the efficacy of cold showers, he adjusted the water until it ran at little more than blood temperature. "You know full well that we are," he said, rinsing them both off. "But this time, we'll take it slowly."

And they did. Slow and easy, with a fire burning in the hearth, and brandy to sip between caresses, and the bed soft beneath them. With leisurely delight and the sort of murmured words a man and a woman exchange when they find untold pleasure in each other.

He explored her from head to foot. Tasted the wild honey of her response as her body yielded to his seduction. Held her tight as she splintered with passion. And when she begged for mercy and whimpered that she could not...*could not* reach orgasm again, he drove himself deep inside her and taught her that, with him, she could.

When at last she fell asleep, some time after midnight, he did not think it likely that she dreamed of the absent Mark.

*   *   *

Light, too bright, too persistent, speared her eyelids and had her squinting into the pillows. Her limbs lay heavy with delicious lassitude. Her mouth felt slightly swollen, her skin a little chafed. She ached pleasurably in hidden places, the way she'd always thought a woman might when she'd been thoroughly loved.

Had she…?

With *Edmund*…?

Or was she still caught in the web of an unusually vivid dream?

Tentatively, her hand stole out to verify reality, checking the other half of the bed. Finding the dent in the other pillow where another head had lain. She stretched her leg under the covers, explored with her toe the barely perceptible warmth of other feet recently removed from the mattress.

As if floodgates had suddenly burst open, memory rushed in.

Cautiously, she opened one eye and took quick inventory of the room. Like hers, it overlooked the Pacific. The cold ashes of last night's fire lay in the hearth. The empty brandy snifters still stood on the bedside table. But of the man who'd brought her to the edge of delirium with his mouth and left her sobbing for release; who'd filled her with his vitality and ridden with her to heights of pleasure she'd never before experienced, not once but over and over again throughout the night—of him there was no sign.

Clutching the duvet to her, she sat up. A thick terry-cloth robe lay across the foot of the bed. Someone had folded her clothes and left them over the arm of a chair, with her shoes neatly placed on the floor below them. The bathroom door stood ajar with no light showing from the interior. Clearly, he wasn't in there.

With a tiny click which seemed deafening in the silent room, the digital clock beside the bed rolled to eight-thirty. How could she have slept so late? How could she have slept *at all?*

By exhausting herself, physically and emotionally until she was as limp as a rag! By curling up next to Edmund's hard, warm frame, sated in body and soul, and refusing to think about what yesterday had brought or what tomorrow might hold because, right at that moment, with nothing but a silver dollar moon to witness the event, the here and now had been enough.

Of course, what they'd shared wasn't love. It couldn't be. Because she loved Mark.

Didn't she?

Of course she did! But he'd deserted her and left her at the mercy of self-doubt and a hurt so deeply wounding that she'd wanted to crawl into a hole and never again come out. Instead, she'd turned to Edmund and, miraculously, passion had flared between them with scorching intensity. Because of him, she'd begun the long process of restoring her confidence in herself as a woman.

Recognizing that was a blessing she'd never expected to find. She knew now that, in time, she would recover. The rest of her life would not be blighted because Mark Armstrong had reneged on his promise to marry her. A whole different world from the one he'd offered waited to be discovered. And one day, when she was ready, she would find a better and a truer love. In the meantime, there was Edmund, and today, and perhaps even tonight.

Sliding her legs to the floor, she reached for the robe and was securing the belt around her waist when a knock came at the door.

"Well," she said, a rush of anticipation warming her cheeks as she ran to open it, "there's no need to be so polite! It's your room, after all!"

A uniformed busboy stood outside, holding a tray. "Your breakfast, ma'am," he announced pleasantly. "May I come in?"

Breakfast for one, she noticed with mild dismay, waving him across the threshold.

Placing the tray on a table by the window, he drew up a chair and removed the fluted paper cover from a tall glass of orange juice. "Another lovely morning, ma'am. A number of our guests are already enjoying the beach."

Of course! And Edmund was probably one of them.

"May I pour your coffee?"

"I'll wait a while, thanks."

"In that case, I'll leave you to enjoy your meal. No," he insisted, backing toward the door when she reached for her purse to tip him, "that's already been taken care of, ma'am. Have a very nice day."

She thought it entirely possible that she would—an amazing concept, all things considered. The rich aroma of coffee underscored by the delicate scent of the single bud rose which completed her breakfast tray, added to the stunning view from the window and the stream of sunlight slanting over the polished wood floor surely made for a great start to the morning.

Buoyed with sudden optimism, she picked up the glass of juice and silently toasted the bright morning. Life really did go on, one day at a time. Trite, perhaps, but true. The secret was to look forward, instead of back.

She did not find Edmund on the beach, nor in the lounge where guests were taking morning coffee when she returned to The Inn two hours later. The Navigator was not in the parking lot. The message light was not blinking on the phone in her room.

"Mr. Delaney checked out early this morning," the clerk told her when, with a growing sense of unease, she inquired at the front desk.

"Checked out?" But he'd told her he was staying for a

week. He'd slept with her the night before. He'd ordered breakfast for her. She'd thought…she'd thought…

What? That a new love could be so easily born to replace the one she'd lost? In fairy tales, perhaps—or the mind of a self-delusional fool!

Still, she looked for a reason that at least hinted of a happy ending. "And you're sure he left no message?"

"He was in a hurry," the clerk said kindly. "I was already on duty when the call came through. Normally, we don't intrude on our guests when they've specifically requested us not to do so, but his wife insisted he be contacted right away—some sort of emergency, I understand. Fortunately, he happened to come into the lobby just then—he'd been down at the pool for an early swim, I believe—and I was able to convey the message right away."

Wife? She'd spent the night in the arms of another woman's *husband?* No wonder he'd phoned the front desk the minute he'd closed his door behind them, and asked not to be disturbed! Risking a call from his wife while he was in bed with another woman would have seriously hampered his performance!

Jenna thought she was going to be sick, right there on the floor in full view of whoever happened to be passing by.

The clerk seemed to think so, too. "Are you feeling unwell, ma'am? Shall I send for a doctor…?"

"No," she said, somehow managing to articulate a response even though her insides were shaking. "Thank you for your concern but I'm perfectly fine."

Dazed with shock, she reeled toward the front door and the cool fresh air outside.

I come with too much excess baggage, he'd said, the night before, but she'd never for a moment supposed he was talking about a wife. He'd seemed too straightforward for such arcane half-truths.

And she…she had only herself to blame for the guilt and

regret now hemming her in on all sides. It was one thing to accept the end of a relationship, and quite another to imagine that flinging herself headlong into the start of another was any solution. New hopes weren't built on the ashes of broken dreams. A person had to heal before she was ready to begin again with someone new.

Furious to find tears brimming yet again, Jenna drew in a shaking breath and squared her shoulders. So, okay! She'd made a mistake. But the damage was done and no amount of weeping and wailing was going to change it. At the very least, she could stop compounding her problems, instead of adding to them.

Her life, her future, lay elsewhere and this place...oh, it had provided the refuge she'd needed during those first long, dreadful hours after she'd received Mark's letter, but at best it was a temporary reprieve only. Sooner or later, she had to go back and face the people and situation she'd left behind.

As for Edmund Delaney, in all fairness, her anger toward him should be tempered by gratitude. Unquestionably, he'd deceived her, but he'd also made her feel desirable again. And for that, she owed him a debt he could never begin to imagine.

"You know," Valerie Sinclair said, regarding Jenna through narrowed eyes, "I don't think it's necessarily over with Mark. If you hadn't disappeared off the face of the earth so suddenly the way you did, I truly believe you'd be married to him by now. He's phoned here, you know. Several times. Says he's tried phoning you as well, but you never return his calls. From what I can gather, he got cold feet at the last minute but he came to his senses soon after."

During the month since her return to Vancouver, Jenna had fielded an endless outpouring of sympathy and numerous offers to hook her up with a new man. She'd refused every one, not because she didn't appreciate the concern of her friends but because she was actually enjoying being free to do and wear and eat what she pleased. Not until he was out of her life had she realized how completely Mark had tried to control it—or how close he'd come to succeeding.

But nothing stopped her mother from harping on the subject of a reconciliation. As far as she was concerned, there was only one avenue worth pursuing, one which led directly back to Mark Armstrong.

Thanking providence and modern technology for the luxury of call display and voice mail, Jenna heaved a weary sigh. "And I've told you, Mother, I have nothing to say to him. Nor can I imagine why you have, either. He humiliated everyone in this family, not just me. And his excuse that he got cold feet is pathetic. He's thirty-one, for heaven's sake, not seventeen!"

"We'd see our way to forgiving him," her mother said magnanimously.

Only because of what you expected he'd do for you, once I became his wife! Jenna muttered silently.

Collecting her jacket and purse, she said, "Forget it, Mother. It's over between Mark and me. Thanks for the coffee, but I really can't stay for lunch. I have a living to earn."

"If you were Mrs. Armstrong, you wouldn't need to rely on the pittance you make running that day-care outfit," her mother persisted.

Jenna rolled her eyes in exasperation. "In case you've forgotten, *Mark's* the one who dumped me! Even supposing you're right and he's undergone yet another change of heart, whatever makes you think I'd be interested in renewing a relationship with a man I could never trust again?"

"So what are you going to do instead? Spend the rest of your life wiping the noses of other people's children?"

"I can think of worse things," she said. *Like finding I*

can't forget the married man I slept with, or realizing Mark's prowess as a lover leaves as much to be desired as just about everything else I've learned about him! "I love working with children, you know that."

And they were one thing Mark's money couldn't buy. An attack of mumps when he was twenty-five had left him sterile. Although she'd found it difficult at first, she'd come to accept that she'd never know how it felt to be pregnant or give birth, and had pinned her hopes instead on persuading him to consider adopting a child when the time was right.

"Come for dinner on Sunday," her mother said, walking her to the door. "The whole family will be here and we've hardly seen you since you came back to town."

"Only if you promise you won't harp on the idea of a reconciliation with Mark. It isn't going to happen, Mother, no matter how badly you'd like it to."

"You're surely not going to pretend you're over him already?"

Could it possibly be? Was that why her thoughts turned so often to Edmund Delaney? "I still think about him occasionally," she admitted.

Her mother beamed with satisfaction. "You miss him!"

The guy's pure pond scum, sweet pea....!

"I'm angry with him."

...sent someone else to do his dirty work? He's not fit to be called a man...

"And disgusted at the way he's behaved."

"You're overwrought because you're in denial, dear."

"I'm tired because I've spent hours sending back wedding gifts to people, well over half of whom I don't know. On top of that, his mother wrote asking me to return my engagement ring—as if I had any use for it, or would dream of keeping an heirloom belonging to another family!"

"Anger and denial are part of the grieving process,"

Valerie said soothingly. "They'll pass, and then you'll feel like your old self again and see things differently."

Was not menstruating and being unable to keep her breakfast down also part of the grieving process, Jenna wondered, staring at her pallid reflection in the bathroom mirror, one morning five weeks later. And would they, too, pass and leave her feeling like her old self?

Or should she just face the fact that nothing was ever going to be the same again. Because while contraception might not have been an issue with Mark, unless she was sadly mistaken, it definitely should have been with Edmund Delaney!

"I think I'm pregnant," she blurted out wretchedly, when Irene, her partner at the day-care center, stopped by that same evening to see how she was coping with the summer cold she'd claimed had prevented her from showing up at work the last couple of days.

It took a lot to rattle Irene. Tantrums, toilet training, finding herself splattered with paint and food—she took them all in stride. "That's the way kids are," she always said. "They spit up on your best blouse and wait till they're sitting on your lap before they wet their pants. It's the nature of the little beasts, but we love them anyway."

Her reaction to Jenna's announcement would have been no less pragmatic had it not been for the spark of curiosity she couldn't quite hide. "Well, it's not Mark's because we both know he was shooting blanks," she said, fixing Jenna in a beady-eyed stare. "So who's the lucky daddy?"

"Someone I…met."

"Well, I didn't think you'd received an anonymous donation in the mail, Jenna! What's his name?"

"It doesn't matter. I'm no longer involved with him."

"*Were* you at the time you were supposed to be getting married? Is that why Mark called off the wedding?"

"Of course not!" she exclaimed, stung. "How could you even ask such a question?"

"It's been known to happen. One last fling before settling down, and all that sort of thing, you know. Men do it all the time, so why not women?"

"Well, not this woman," Jenna said, afraid she was about to lose the dry toast and scrambled egg she'd forced down earlier.

Irene subjected her to another inspection. "You do look a bit off-color, I must admit, but it doesn't have to mean you're pregnant."

"To what else would you attribute two missed periods and morning sickness which lasts all day?"

"Stress, for one thing. What you've been through in the last couple of months is enough to put any woman's cycle out of kilter," Irene replied, a shade more sympathetically. "But if you're right, you've got to know I'm not the only person who'll wonder if this is the reason Mark backed out at the last minute. People are going to have a field day with this one, sweet child!"

"I'm past caring what other people think," Jenna said wearily. "I've got a life that I thought was sorting itself out rather well. Now I'm back at square one again and facing questions a lot more important than what's making the gossip vine thrive."

"Hmm." Irene nibbled on a fingernail. "How far along do you think you are?"

"Nine weeks." *Plus one day and nineteen hours, to be precise!*

"Have you thought about what you want to do?"

"Do?"

"You don't have to go through with the pregnancy, Jenna. There are other options."

"I hope you're not hinting at an abortion," she said, shocked. "I was reconciled to never having children with

Mark. I've accepted his leaving me standing at the altar. But this…*this* is *my* baby and I'm damned if I'll let anyone rob me of him—or her!''

''What about the father's rights?''

''The father has no rights,'' she spat, jumping up from her chair and pacing agitatedly across the room and back. ''I haven't seen or heard from him since the night we…had sex.''

Because he already has a wife.

''Don't get your knickers in an uproar,'' Irene said calmly. ''Whatever you decide, I'm with you all the way, you know that. You can work as much or as little as you like before the birth. And after, when you feel up to it, you can come back to the center and bring the munchkin with you. If single parenthood's the route you choose to go, you've got the ideal setup. No need to worry about baby-sitters or leaving him with strangers.''

She made it all sound so possible. And maybe it would have remained that way if, that following Sunday night, Edmund Delaney hadn't shown up on Jenna's doorstep.

''I've had a devil of a time tracking you down,'' he said, when she opened the door. ''You're not listed in the phone book, you never did tell me your last name, and if it hadn't been that the desk clerk at The Inn was susceptible to a bribe, I never would have found you. You look like hell, by the way.''

Appalled, she stared at him, willing him to be a figment of her nauseated imagination. In the beginning, she'd fantasized more than was good for her about what might have happened if he hadn't been married and they'd spent a few more days together. But common sense had finally prevailed and she'd long since accepted that, in his own way, Edmund was no better than Mark and she was well rid of both of them.

He was looking at her quizzically, his slate-blue eyes with

their absurdly long lashes sparkling with laughter. "Aren't you going to invite me in, sweet pea?"

"No," she said. "Go away. And I'm not your sweet pea."

But before she could slam it in his face, he had his foot in the door, and then the rest of him. "Hey," he said, "I know you're probably ticked with me, but I can explain."

Ignoring the lurching of her stomach, she straightened to her full height and glared at him, sincerely believing she was in charge of herself and her emotions. "Nothing you have to say excuses your behavior. You are...you are...!"

"Pond scum?" A grin tugged at his mouth and he had the audacity to reach out and cup her chin.

His hand was warm and strong and steady; the kind that made a woman feel safe and protected and all those things she badly needed to see her through the coming months and years. And knowing she couldn't have them—at least not from him—had her suddenly choking back the tears which, along with all the other less than welcome symptoms of pregnancy, plagued her without warning.

"I would have come before," he said gravely, seeing her distress. "But I've been away and only just got back. How are you, Jenna, my dear?"

Pregnant, that's how! And just to prove it, the soup she'd had for dinner rose up in her throat with alarming urgency. Blindly, she spun away from him and headed for the bathroom at the end of the hall.

CHAPTER FOUR

SHE had no idea he'd followed her, that he saw her hunched over the toilet bowl and heard her retching, until she felt him scooping the hair away from her face and pressing a cold cloth to her forehead.

"Ugh…!" she gagged, swatting ineffectually at him. "Leave me…alone…!"

He stroked her back as another spasm took hold. "Not a chance," he said. "You ought to know by now that I can't ignore a lady in distress."

"I will not have you see me like this!"

"From where I stand, sweet pea, you're in no position to be issuing orders. You've got your work cut out tossing your cookies."

The man was about as sensitive as a water buffalo. "Show a little tact, for pity's sake! I don't need an…audience."

"Instead of fighting me every step of the way," he said virtuously, "you might try thanking me for showing up when I did, since it's obvious to anyone with two neurons to rub together that you could use a little help."

She crawled to a sitting position on the lip of the bathtub as the bout of sickness abated. "Sorry to disappoint you, but I'm fresh out of gratitude where you're concerned."

He rinsed the cloth in more cold water and attempted to wipe her flushed face. "No call to get testy, Jenna. You aren't the first woman I've seen throw up and I suspect you won't be the last."

She slapped his hand away. "Stop fussing over me! I'm feeling better."

He inspected her minutely, starting with her bare feet

52

sticking out at the bottom of her ratty old pink bathrobe, and ending with her hair which hadn't seen the working end of a brush in hours. "You look like the wrath of God!"

"So you keep telling me."

"Worse even than you did the night we met."

"Thank you," she said peevishly.

"Is it something you ate that's making you ill?"

"Yes," she lied, because to admit the truth to him, of all people, was out of the question.

"You want me to put you to bed?"

"God, no!" She sprang up from the edge of the tub and tried to push past him. "You've already done enough damage!"

She didn't need his raised eyebrows and quizzical expression to know she'd almost blown her cover.

"How so, Jenna?" he asked carefully, manacling her wrist in an iron grip. "What heinous crime have I committed, beyond making a habit of being there to pick up the pieces when things go wrong in your life?"

She attempted to stare him down, which was a mistake. For a start, he didn't stare down easily. And second, he was too disturbingly good-looking. Admiring his face, with its strong, clean lines, led to her remembering other, equally chiseled parts of him, and that provoked exactly the kind of turbulence her stomach was in no shape to tolerate. "I'm surprised you have the nerve to ask me that!"

"If you're referring to the night we spent together, let me remind you that I made a superhuman effort to decline the invitation you so charmingly extended."

"Oh!" she gasped, a furious blush riding up her neck at the unquestionable truth of his allegation. "Only an utter boor would throw that back in my face!"

His hold on her wrist lessened, became a lazy, evocative caress. "Before you fly into orbit, let me also say that I found it a memorably magnificent experience which I have never for a moment regretted.''

"Did you really?" she snapped, refusing to be blindsided by his belated attempt at flattery. "Is that why you left so early the next morning without so much as a note telling me why?"

"Funny you should mention that since it's one of the reasons I felt obliged to track you down now. Believe me, Jenna, I'm well aware I have some explaining to do.'' He trailed his fingers over her palm, folded her hand around his, and propelled her toward the door. "But if it's all the same to you, I'd as soon find some place more conducive to conversation before I unburden myself. Unless, of course, you think you might be sick again any time soon?"

Annoyed to find herself warming to his touch, she wrenched her hand away. "I already told you, I'm feeling much better."

"Enough to offer me coffee?"

She hadn't been able to tolerate coffee for days. The mere mention of it was enough to leave her salivating like a rabid dog. "I'm out of coffee."

"Beer, then?"

"I don't drink beer."

He compressed his rather beautiful mouth, though whether it was to contain a grimace or a grin she couldn't decide. "Okay, Jenna, you choose. And if acting the perfect hostess strains your energy too severely, I'll be happy to take over in the kitchen and do the honors myself."

"I wouldn't dream of it," she said, resigned to the fact that she wasn't going to be rid of him until he was good and ready to leave of his own accord. "I can offer you ginger ale or tea. Take your pick."

"How gracious! I'll settle for tea, thanks."

She indicated the living room to the left of the front hall. "Have a seat in there then, while I make it."

She was just as glad he hadn't asked for ginger ale. At least waiting for the kettle to boil for tea allowed her time to scurry to her bedroom, abandon the pink bathrobe for a silk jersey caftan, unearth a pair of high-heeled satin slippers, and rake a brush through her hair. Most definitely *not* to impress Mr. Married-Man Edmund Delaney, she assured her pasty-faced image in the mirror, but to make herself feel human again. She hadn't needed his candid assessment to know she looked as if she'd just been dug up!

He hadn't been idly twiddling his thumbs during the time she was gone, either. When she carried the tea tray into the living room, she saw that he'd turned on a table lamp and was leafing through a photograph album he'd found in her bookcase. "Do make yourself at home," she said sourly.

"I already have," he returned, not the least bit perturbed at being caught snooping. "Is this the chinless wonder you almost married?"

She cast a quick glance at the picture in question. "It is. And while you might not think so, most people find Mark very handsome."

Edmund snorted irreverently. "I guess—if you're into roosters! Quite a beak he's sporting, wouldn't you say?"

"Is that why you showed up tonight?" she asked, depositing the tray on the coffee table with more force than was good for either. "To belittle someone who once played a very important role in my life, and so make me out to be an even bigger idiot than I already am?"

He slapped the album closed and replaced it on the shelf. "No, sweet pea, that's not my style, though I don't mind admitting to a certain curiosity about him. I already told you one reason I'm here is to apologize for pulling a disappearing act on the Island, the way I did. The other is to see how you're coping in the aftermath of being left at the church door."

"Perfectly well, thank you. And it seems to me that you

should save your apologies for the person who most deserves them.''

''Huh?''

She poured the tea and handed him a cup. ''I'm referring to your wife, Edmund, though I suppose you can be excused for forgetting you have one, given your penchant for infidelity.''

If his surprise wasn't real, he gave an excellent imitation of the genuine article. ''What the devil are you talking about, Jenna?'' he exclaimed, practically slopping his tea into his lap. ''I'm not married!''

''Really?'' she said, regarding him levelly over the rim of her cup. ''Then how would you describe yourself, given that some woman claiming to be your wife called The Inn and left a message which was urgent enough to make you cut short your holiday and leave me feeling like a one-night floozy?''

''That was my *ex-wife,* Adrienne.''

The only cause for Jenna's heart to give a joyful little leap at his disclosure was relief at learning she hadn't been party to adultery. She would admit to no other possible explanation!

''And the reason I left so suddenly,'' Edmund went on grimly, ''is that my four-year-old daughter had been seriously injured in a farming accident.''

''Oh…!'' Dismay and embarrassment eclipsed her brief elation like storm clouds chasing away the sun. ''Oh, Edmund, I'm so sorry! Is she…?''

''She's going to be fine, but it's been a tough haul. That's what's kept me away so long. I wanted to stay close until she was over the worst.''

''Well, of course! Any parent would.'' Not wishing her next question to sound indelicate, she phrased her words carefully. ''Will there be any permanent…consequences?''

''The doctors say not, though whether they're right remains to be seen. But it's the emotional trauma she's suffered that concerns me. And her future safety.''

Every self-protective instinct Jenna possessed urged her not to get any more involved with this man than she already had. Her life was complicated enough. But when she'd hit rock bottom, he was the one she'd run to and he hadn't turned her away.

He'd made her laugh when she'd thought she'd never laugh again. He dried her tears. And he'd loved her, if only for one night.

No laughter curved his mouth now, though. No wicked amusement lurked in his eyes. His face, his posture, the way he ran his finger inside the collar of his sport shirt as if it were strangling him, the heavy sigh he couldn't quite disguise, spoke of a man—a *parent*—beset by worry. And that changed everything.

It brought home in a very real way her own impending role in a child's life. She'd never expected to fall pregnant, least of all by a man she barely knew. But now that it had happened, she couldn't bring herself to regret it.

Despite the gossip and speculation she knew lay ahead, not to mention the unsought advice, she wanted this baby more than anything she'd ever wanted in her life. She loved it with all the fierce, protective passion of a tigress guarding her cub. How she would survive if something happened to her child, if tragedy were to strike him or her, she couldn't begin to imagine. It would kill her!

As if what had befallen Edmund's daughter might somehow communicate itself to her own little one, Jenna found herself unconsciously shielding her womb with her hand. ''Why do you think she isn't safe, Edmund?''

''She's playing where she shouldn't be, wandering around unsupervised. And her mother's too busy trying to be the perfect country man's wife to remember that her first responsibility is to the child left over from a marriage gone sour.''

''Are you saying you blame your ex-wife for the accident?''

''I blame her and her husband! He should have been more careful! A four-year-old needs to be watched constantly, not left to run free wherever she pleases, especially not when there's heavy machinery around. She damn near lost both her legs because no one was looking out for her!''

The tea Jenna had consumed lurched unpleasantly in her stomach and threatened to rise up in her throat. Horrified, she clapped a hand to her mouth.

''Hey, sweet pea, don't get all choked up,'' Edmund said, his tone gentling. ''It didn't happen. Molly's making a good recovery, and I'm going to see to it she isn't put at risk like that again. Just because I'm not married to her mother doesn't change the fact that I'll always be her father, and I'm not about to settle for a secondary role in my child's life. I intend to assert my parental rights to the full.''

So possessively passionate a declaration made Jenna's blood run a little cold. How would he react if he found out he'd fathered more than one child? Would he insist on his full parental rights regarding that child, too? Perhaps even try to relegate *her* to a less prominent role in her baby's life, to compensate for what he'd already lost?

The mere idea made her feel ill all over again. On the surface, he came across as a man eminently reasonable and just, yet she sensed that, if stirred to anger, he would make a formidable opponent.

But what she *knew* was that having him as an ally had helped her through the darkest hours of her life. He'd been her champion when she had no one else to turn to. Because of him, she'd emerged from her own misfortunes all the stronger. Given that, and the knowledge that his learning the truth would not, after all, destroy a marriage, was she being fair to keep her pregnancy a secret from him?

Nervously, she smoothed her right hand over the fingers of her left. The answers were no longer as clear-cut as she'd once thought, and she wished he'd leave so that she could be alone and sort out her thoughts.

"You do that a lot you know," Edmund said.

She looked up, puzzled. "Do what?"

"Trace your thumb over the place where you used to wear Armstrong's ring."

"Really?"

"Really. Still crying yourself to sleep every night over him?"

"Absolutely not! He's out of my life."

"You almost sound as if you mean that."

"I do," she said emphatically.

She'd been making the same claim for weeks and couldn't have said when it had shifted from proud denial to relieved truth. There hadn't been a thunderclap to mark the day or moment. It was more that distance had not lent Mark enchantment. Instead, it had stripped him of his carefully cultivated mystique and revealed such inherent weaknesses that she had been able to let him go without regret.

Now, other events—her baby, motherhood—filled the space in her heart which once he'd occupied. "He wasn't as crucial to my happiness as I believed," she said. "In fact, I'm enjoying being my own person again."

"That's good," Edmund said. "I'm glad."

"I wish more people shared your opinion! I'm forever being set up to meet someone new. My friends refuse to believe I'm happy being unattached, and as for my family…!" She shook her head disbelievingly. "They think the breakup is the tragedy of the decade and I should try to get back together with him, if you can imagine."

"And you'd never consider the possibility?"

"Never. It's out of the question." *For a reason you can't begin to imagine!*

"Then I don't need to worry about you anymore." He smothered a yawn and got to his feet. "I should push off. You're looking a bit peaked again, Jenna, and I've had a long day."

An hour before, she'd have said he never should have come to begin with. Now, surprisingly, she found herself reluctant to see him go. "It was nice of you to stop by."

"That's me, all right...Mr. Nice Guy!" He closed in on her and for one wild, exhilarating moment, she thought he was going to try to kiss her. Instead, he smiled and cuffed her gently under the chin. "I'll stay in touch."

From the third-floor balcony off her living room, she watched him leave the apartment building and cut across the lawn to the street where the Navigator was parked. He walked with a long, easy stride, a tall, dark and handsome man who exerted a powerful fascination for her above and beyond the fact that he'd fathered the child she carried.

Mark had taught her the hard way that men weren't always what they seemed, yet she found herself wanting to believe in Edmund and to trust him. Which brought her back to the question which had been hammering to be heard since he'd told her he was no longer married: dare she risk telling him he was the father of her unborn child? Or should she play it safe and sever all connection with him?

More confused by the minute, she backed into the living room and closed the glass doors to the balcony. Her faith in her own judgment had been badly shaken by the fiasco with Mark. She needed to discuss her predicament with someone clear-sighted enough to see the big picture, and unbiased enough to offer an impartial opinion. She needed to talk to her best friend, Irene.

"What I'd do," Irene decided the next day, while the toddlers napped in the shade of the cherry tree in the day-care center's back garden, and the older children played in the sandbox, "is wait to see if he contacts you again. If he doesn't, the message coming through loud and clear is that the guy's not interested in pursuing…whatever it is the two of you have going, and you'd be asking for trouble if you'd tried to force the issue."

"And if he does call?"

"Play it by ear. Heck, Jenna, you know the drill—ask him why his marriage failed, scope him out about having more children some day, get him to tell you more about his work, his lifestyle."

"More?" Jenna's laugh was strained. "I don't know the first thing about his work or where he lives or what he does in his spare time. I don't know how old he is, where he was born, whether he has all his own teeth, if he's an only child or one of ten, a foundling, an heir…*I don't know the man,* period!"

"Seems to me you've got some homework to do then, before you even think about springing the news that he's going to be a daddy again. You've been through enough this year, Jenna, without winding up with another loser."

"But it's his baby! Don't you think he has the right to know that?"

"Look around you," Irene said. "More than half these children spend their days with us because their mothers are out working full-time, and why is that?"

"They have no place else to leave them."

"Right. The women married deadbeats who didn't stick around to carry their share of the load so that mommy could stay home and look after her kids herself. How often have we heard those same women say that today's the day the father's supposed to pick his child up after work and spend some 'quality' time with him? And how often have we had to phone Mom to say Dad was a no-show, and her little guy's huddled in a corner, sobbing his heart out with disappointment?''

"Too often.''

"Exactly! So no, I don't think this Edmund Delaney has the right to know a thing, just because he happened to get you pregnant. You've got to be sure he's willing to go one step further and be a father as well, before you invite him to get involved in raising the child. If he's not, spare yourself the possibility of unpleasant complications down the road.''

Jenna agreed with everything Irene had said—except for one part. Every child deserved to know his father if it was remotely possible, and she wasn't willing to risk denying her baby that opportunity by leaving matters to chance. When a week passed and she still hadn't heard from Edmund, she took matters into her own hands, looked up his number in the phone book, and called to invite him to dinner the following Friday.

She lived in an older apartment near English Bay, one with high ceilings and fancy molding around the doors and windows. The mantel over her fireplace was Edwardian, the light fixture in her dining room classic art deco, the leaded windows of a quality not to be found today. They'd immediately caught his eye, the first time he'd seen them, and were one reason he'd been happy to fall in with her suggestion that they get together again. He was interested in the history of the building and any plans that might be underway for modernizing it.

The other reason was to make sure she'd recovered from food poisoning. Nothing more. She wasn't ready for another heavy-duty relationship and even if she were, he wasn't the man for the job. But that didn't mean they couldn't engage in a purely platonic relationship.

Parking was tight along her street but he'd driven the convertible that night and managed to squeeze it into a parking spot better suited to a motorcycle. She'd said seven, and it was only ten to, so he took his time strolling through the gates and past lush gardens planted with old-fashioned roses to the stone portico at the main entrance of her building.

She buzzed him inside the building so promptly that he figured she must have spotted him coming up the drive, yet when she opened her door, she seemed strangely flustered. "Oh…Edmund! You're here! Already…!"

"Hello, Jenna. You're looking better," he said, putting her manner down to the fact that he'd shown up ten minutes early. "Not nearly as green around the gills as you were last week."

In fact, she looked stunning. Not that he pretended to be any fashion expert but he knew what he liked and in his view, too many women were blinded by designer labels, regardless of the clothes attached to them. But she'd got it just right in a light blue sleeveless dress belted at the waist. He liked her shoes, too. Pretty, feminine things, instead of the trench hoppers so may women seemed to go for lately. Made him glad he'd decided to wear a jacket and tie, even though his usual preference ran to something more casual.

"Do come in," she said, massaging her ring finger nervously. "It's such a lovely evening, I thought we might sit on the balcony for a while and…chat." She indicated a brass tea wagon set up as a bar, with a couple of decanters, bottled water, a bucket of ice and dish of sliced lime, then scurried away from him as if he had a communicable disease. "Help yourself to a drink while I take care of a couple of last-minute things in the kitchen."

"May I fix something for you?"

Her voice floated back down the hall. "I'll stick with Perrier, thanks."

He poured himself a scotch and wandered out to the balcony. She'd grouped antique wicker furniture around little stone urns filled with scarlet geraniums and some sort of blue trailing flower. A wrought iron stand about three feet high held six fat candles. At the far end of the balcony, positioned where it would catch the afternoon sun, was a padded chaise with a small fountain beside it.

Nice. Very nice—except for the tension which hung in the air like invisible fog. Something wasn't right about the whole setup, and if he'd had any doubts about it, she put paid to them when she eventually came out to join him.

Perching gingerly on the edge of her chair like a bird ready to take flight at the first hint of danger, she launched into painful conversation, although he might as well not have been there for all the eye contact they exchanged. "Well, here we are," she said woodenly, addressing the wall behind him.

"Indeed."

"I made lemon chicken. I hope you like it."

"I'm pretty easy to please when it comes to food."

"The weather's been wonderful, hasn't it?"

"Wonderful."

Her glance skittered past him and settled on the trees lining the street. "Exceptionally dry, even for July."

"I guess."

She sipped her Perrier, set the glass down on the low table between their chairs, and started drawing imaginary rings on her finger. Again. "They're forecasting a long, hot summer."

Okay, he'd had enough! "When two people can't find anything else to talk about but the weather, it's usually an indication that they're not having a very good time. Are you wishing you hadn't asked me here tonight, Jenna?"

That caught her off guard enough that she locked gazes with him and if he hadn't known better, he'd have said she was on the verge of panic. "N-no!"

"Then why don't you just relax and enjoy my company?"

Like a diver about to plunge into a very deep pool, she

drew in a breath which made her breasts heave, and said, "Because I have an ulterior motive for inviting you. I need to ask you something."

"So, fire away," he said. "What do you want to know?"

He wasn't sure what he expected—something that needed fixing in the apartment, possibly—and so was completely unprepared when she started quizzing him as if he were running for public office and might have a dirty secret in his past.

"For a start," she said, "where do you live?"

"Near Lost Lagoon."

"In an apartment?"

"Yeah," he said, "but it's nothing near as interesting as your place."

"Have you always lived downtown?"

Without a clue as to where all this was leading, he shook his head. "Uh-uh. I owned a house in West Vancouver when Adrienne and I were together."

"Which do you prefer?"

"A house made sense when I was married, especially once Molly was born, but an apartment's easier now that I'm single again." Mystified, he tossed her a quizzical glance. "What's with the third degree, Jenna?"

"I'm interested in you, that's all."

"I'm flattered—I think."

She brushed that aside as if it were of no consequence how he felt, and started off down another avenue. "How is Molly?"

"Doing well, thanks."

"Do you get to see her very often?"

"Not nearly as much as I'd like. Adrienne's husband owns a vineyard in the Okanagan, down near Osoyoos, which is a fair drive from Vancouver as I'm sure you know. Anything else?"

"Yes," she said, as if she were mentally ticking items off a list. "Why did your marriage end?"

He frowned and set down his glass. He'd always fancied himself pretty good at steering a conversation in the direction he wanted it to go, but he was beginning to think he'd met his match in her. "Why do you care?"

"Well, you already know plenty about me," she said, all big, innocent eyes and artless demeanor, neither of which had him fooled for a minute. There was a lot more going on here than she was telling! "So it seems a fair exchange that you tell me something about you. Unless, of course, you have something to hide."

"Not a darn thing, sweet pea," he said, adopting the same guileless expression she was working so hard to maintain. "Adrienne was from a small town not far from where she's living now. She came to Vancouver because she thought the big city would be more glamorous and exciting. We met, fell in love, made plans, got married, and had a baby, in that order. In other words, did all the right things for what appeared to be the right reasons."

"So what went wrong?"

"Ultimately, our goals and expectations didn't mesh. She found it too lonely staying home with a baby all day and started making noises about us moving closer to her parents. But I had a business to run here so I suggested she go home and spend a couple of days with her family every once in a while. Once in a while turned into every second week, though, and next she started hinting that, since I was out at work Monday through Friday, she might as well just come back here on the weekends. The feelings—love, if you like—changed, eventually died, our marriage went down the tubes, she met someone else better able to give her the kind of life she wanted, and married him."

"Just like that?"

"No," he said, beginning to get irritated. "Not just like

that. Relationships aren't built in a day and they don't break down that fast, either. A lot of resentment and a whole whack of guilt enter the picture, especially when a child's involved. So if you're asking me if I have any regrets, the answer's yes. I regret not having my daughter live with me. I resent the fact that she lives too far away for me to see her every day, to read to her at bedtime, to take her to the park. And it drives me nuts to know she's calling some other man 'Daddy.' Does that answer all your questions?''

"Not quite.''

He heaved a sigh and shook his head. "I could be home in the peace and quiet of my own apartment, doing nothing more strenuous than watching TV,'' he informed the world at large. "Why did I think coming here instead was a good idea?''

"I'm sorry,'' she said, her face the picture of remorse. "I wish there was some other way to do this.''

"Do what, for crying out loud? Where are all these questions leading?''

She hopped out of her chair as if she'd just found herself sharing space with a pit viper, and if she'd been edgy before, she was verging on nervous hysteria now. "I'll tell you, I will! As soon as you tell me what you do for a living.''

"I'm gainfully self-employed.''

"Doing what?''

Exasperated, he plunked his glass down and strode to where she stood. "Cripes, Jenna!'' he snapped. "Is this about how much money I make? Would you like to see my bank statements? Run a credit check on me? Or are you trying to touch me up for a loan?''

She shrank away from him. "No. And I don't mean to pry,'' she mumbled, eyes downcast.

"Gee, you could've fooled me! If there's something I've done that's bugging you, just spit it out and have done with, instead of beating around the bush like this.''

She lifted her gaze to his at that, and he was reminded of a deer caught in the headlights of a trucker's rig speeding down the freeway. She looked trapped and she looked terrified. "I apologize," she said, so contritely that he immediately felt as if he'd just kicked a helpless puppy out into the teeth of a winter storm. "It's just that I don't know how else to go about this."

"Go about what? What the devil's riding you so hard that you're almost hyperventilating? Is Armstrong harassing you, is that it?"

"No," she said in a small voice.

"Then what? Hell, Jenna, just say the words. It's probably not nearly as bad as your imagination's making it out to be."

"Oh, it's bad," she said tremulously. "Because, you see, I'm…pregnant."

CHAPTER FIVE

THE word dropped like a pebble in a pond, the ramifications spreading in ever-expanding circles. As if she hadn't already been through enough, without having this dumped on her...!

"Pregnant?" he echoed, in hushed sympathy, stroking his hands up and down her bare arms. For all that the temperature on the balcony must have been over seventy, she was cold as ice to the touch. "Jeez, small wonder you're in such a state then! Just when you thought your life was your own again, this happens. And I suppose, given his previous track record, that Armstrong's backing away from taking any responsibility?"

Mutely, she stared at him, the glazed, cornered-doe look in her eyes more pronounced than ever. She gulped, tried to speak, and couldn't. Gooseflesh pebbled her skin and she started to shake uncontrollably.

A red fury rode through Edmund. Someone needed to teach Armstrong a lesson and he was just the man for the job! Catching both her hands in his, he said, "Is he trying to coerce you into having an abortion, Jenna? Because if he is, I'll see to it that he—"

"No!" she burst out. "Mark doesn't even...know I'm pregnant."

"Why not?"

"Because," she said.

"Because?" He gave her a little shake. "That's no answer, Jenna. He's got to know. Why haven't you told him?"

She swallowed painfully. "Because," she said again, "it isn't his baby."

Dumbfounded, he stared at her. "Not *his?* Then whose...?

69

She stared right back and didn't say a word.

"Oh, no! *Oh, no!*" He backed away, palms raised in protest, as understanding sank home and the pieces fell into place. "You're not trying to tell me it's mine?"

She looked about ready to keel over. "I'm afraid so."

"What makes you so sure?" he blustered, even as part of his mind was telling him, *Why wouldn't it be yours? You went after her like a randy rabbit and you didn't use anything....*

"Because you're the only one who possibly could be the father."

"Bull!" he said bluntly. "You told me yourself you and Armstrong were lovers. We met when you were supposed to be on your honeymoon. Presumably you were on the pill. And if you weren't, that's even more reason to think that he—"

"There was no need for contraception. Mark can't have children," she said, nailing him straight between the eyes with such utter sincerity that he knew he didn't need medical proof to support her allegation. "He's sterile. So that leaves you as the only other candidate."

For a long moment, heavy silence hung in the air between them, muffling the sounds of the city below. He was aware of his heart thudding, of a bird flitting through the air, of the distant blast of a car horn. And of her, all terrified eyes and quivering mouth.

"Why didn't you say something at the time then?" he finally exploded, fit to tear his hair out. "I could have taken care of things...seen to it this didn't happen!"

"I wasn't thinking straight," she cried, shaken to retaliation by his anger. "If I had been, do you think I would have thrown myself at you the way I did?"

"Oh, *hell!*" Enraged as much with himself as with her, he slammed one fist against the other palm. "If this isn't enough to drive a man to drink!"

"I'm very sorry," she said, her voice breaking. "I know this must be very upsetting for you."

"*Upsetting?*" He spun back to her scornfully. "Try 'shocked,' Jenna! Try 'outraged!' Try 'disbelieving!'"

"I'm telling you the truth, Edmund! I wouldn't lie about a thing like this."

"So how come it took you so long to get around to sharing the happy news? You must be what…ten, eleven weeks along?"

"For a start," she said, "you disappeared. And even if you hadn't, I'd planned not to involve you."

"What changed your mind? Finding out I didn't have a criminal record as long as your arm and could afford to support a child, is that it?"

"I changed my mind when I learned that telling you wouldn't cause your marriage to break up."

"Well, aren't you the noble one!"

"I was trying to do what was best for everyone. I still am. When you showed up last week and told me you were divorced, I thought—"

"What? That it left the field clear for you to move in?"

"No! But it did seem to indicate you were interested in furthering our…relationship."

He heard her sniff, and ventured a glance at her. Worry shadowed her eyes. Her lip quivered like a leaf in a gale. She looked as distraught as the night he'd met her. And look where things had gone from there!

"I need a refill!" he said, raking a frustrated hand through his hair. "I know now why you're sticking to Perrier, but if it's all the same to you, I could use another scotch."

"Help yourself. And if you'd like to be alone for a while, I can make myself scarce in the kitchen. The chicken's probably ready to come out of the oven by now anyway, and I still haven't tossed the salad."

"You running out of the room isn't going to change anything," he informed her, splashing a good inch of liquor into his glass and downing half. "And quite frankly, I've lost my appetite for chicken. As far as I'm concerned, the whole evening's gone down the tubes. Talk about a total screw-up!"

She bit her lip and fiddled around with her ring finger again. She'd pull the damned thing off one day, if she wasn't careful! "I see," she said stiffly. "Well, before you dash off, there's something else I want to tell you."

"You're having triplets," he said with gloomy sarcasm. "Go ahead, Jenna. Hit me with your best shot!"

"No, Edmund," she returned, with such quiet dignity that he wished he'd shown himself capable of one-tenth as much class. "Just this—I finally decided to tell you about the pregnancy not because I expect anything from you that you don't want to give, but because I thought you'd want to know. If my questions tonight seemed intrusive, it was because I was trying to determine how you might react to the news. If I'd had reason to believe you were the kind of man who'd prefer to…remain in ignorance, I'd not have breathed a word. But the way you feel about Molly and your unwillingness to relinquish your parental rights and obligations convinced me you'd want to know about this baby."

"What you really mean is you were testing me to see if I'm fit to have my name on the birth certificate. Hell, Jenna, don't go all diplomatic on me now!"

"All right, I won't. That's exactly what I was trying to find out," she admitted, the guilt and remorse on her face pulverizing his insides. "I'd rather my child have no father at all than one who resents him."

"And good old Delaney passed the test with flying colors!"

"If that's the way you want to look at it, yes."

"Peachy," he said grimly. "So now that that's settled, what do we do next?"

"What do you want to do?"

Raise hell and put a lid on it! Lambaste you for being so damned needy! Kick myself in the rear for being such a prize idiot!

He drew in a deep breath. "This isn't a good time to ask leading questions like that, Jenna."

"Then perhaps," she said, tilting one shoulder in a faint shrug, "the best thing might be for you to leave."

Damn right! In his present state, he was liable to say things better left unsaid and make a bad situation worse. He needed to clear his head, get a handle on things, and he couldn't do either with her big gray eyes fixed on him and gleaming with unshed tears.

"Good idea. I'll…" What? Change history? Fat chance!

He lifted his hand, hoping inspiration would fall out of the sky and he'd find the right words to say. But there weren't any right words. Nothing about the situation was right. He'd screwed up. Badly. He blew out a breath and turned away. "I'll…see you," he finished lamely.

She changed into her old pink bathrobe, and huddled on the chaise on the balcony, and heard the night sink slowly into silence. Saw the windows in nearby buildings grow dark one by one until only patches of light from the street lamps were left. Gazed up at the distant stars and wished there was some way she could latch onto one and begin all over again in a faraway place where no one knew her.

The grandmother clock in the hall struck midnight. One. Two. Three.

Edmund's half-drunk tumbler of scotch remained where he'd left it on the table, just before he'd stormed out. In the kitchen, the overcooked chicken lay cold and congealed in lemon sauce. The table, still set for two, with candles and a vase of yellow rosebuds, stood undisturbed in the dining room.

And her plan, which had seemed so foolproof in theory, had proved disastrous in fact, and been reduced to a shambles. What she'd intended as a tactful probe into his background had turned into a clumsy, insulting interrogation. The calm revelation that she was pregnant had emerged full of unspoken accusation.

Instead of his embracing the news that they'd made a baby together, he'd seen it as a disaster, an attempt to rope him into something he had absolutely no interest in being a part of. He hadn't been able to wait to escape before she sprang another trap.

She stared up at a winking star and tried telling herself it was for the best. If he wasn't prepared to be there for the long haul, better he wasn't there at all. It would be too easy to become dependent on him; too easy to be crushed if he eventually bowed out.

But she was crushed anyway because his reaction had laid bare a truth she hadn't been willing to acknowledge before. When she'd set up tonight's invitation, she'd been hoping for a miracle. Hoping, after the initial shock wore off, that he'd be glad she was having his baby and insist on being part of its life. Instead, he'd done neither and she'd lost a friend.

The realization shredded her courage to coleslaw. If she'd found other people's pity hard to take when Mark left her, how much worse it would surely be when she could no longer keep her pregnancy a secret. *Poor, stupid Jenna!* they'd whisper, with that mixture of compassion and malice another person's misfortunes so often provoked. *Talk about out of the frying pan and into the fire! What next, do you suppose?*

Knowing she had Edmund's support would have made all the difference. With him on her side, the rest of the world could have done its worst and she would have survived. But now…

Too beset to think straight, she leaned her head on her knees and pressed her fingers to her temples. It might have helped if she could cry, but tears were a luxury she couldn't afford. The mess she was in was all of her own making, and weeping wasn't going to clean it up.

Perhaps moving away *was* the answer. A fresh start in some place where no one knew her, where no memories lingered to remind her of the mistakes she'd made, might be best for her and the baby.

Tucking her feet under the hem of her robe, she curled up on her side. Tomorrow, she'd give the idea more thought. Tomorrow when she wasn't so weary, things wouldn't seem so hopeless.

She awoke hours later, thoroughly chilled, numb down one side, and with a cramp in her leg and a mosquito bite on her ankle. Long fingers of sunlight painted shadows on the lawns and turned the dew to spun silver. A phone rang in the next door apartment, the aroma of freshly brewed coffee wafted on the air. And someone was knocking repeatedly at her door.

Bleary-eyed, she hobbled down the hall, squinting at the clock as she passed by. Barely six in the morning and she had a visitor already? Either the building was on fire or else…

Or else it could be Edmund! Given the nature of the unfinished business between them, who else was it likely to be at such an hour?

Her heart was in her throat as she inched open the door.

Unsmiling, with a five o'clock shadow blurring his jaw and eyes ringed with fatigue, he stood on the threshold, cardboard tray holding tall paper cups in one hand, paper bag containing heaven knew what in the other.

"Gad," he said, pushing past her and nudging the door

closed with his hip, "you look even worse than I do! What happened to your face?"

Perplexed, she shot a glance at herself in the gilt mirror hanging on the wall and wished she hadn't bothered. Not only was her right cheek all creased from where she'd spent the night on the chaise, her hair was plastered to the side of her head and her mascara from yesterday had smeared itself halfway to her chin, prompting her spiteful alter ego to inquire spitefully, *Who let you out of your cage, dearie?*

"I wasn't expecting company," she said, surreptitiously wiping a fingertip beneath each eye. "In fact, you woke me up. How did you get in the building, anyway?"

"Some early bird jogger let me in on his way out. And I'm glad one of us had a restful night!"

"I'd hardly call falling asleep just before dawn 'a restful night'!" she snapped, in the face of his unalloyed bad temper. "So if you've come here to berate me some more, you can leave. I don't need you or anyone else telling me what a perfect dolt I am. I already gave myself that lecture a dozen times over."

"Oh, for the love of God!" He rolled his eyes and made a visible effort to collect himself. "Look, I'm here because I was hoping we could talk without getting all exercised. I even brought breakfast as a peace offering, see?" He waved the paper cups under her nose. "Fresh coffee and Danish pastries."

"What's to talk about?" she said, unmollified. "I thought you said all there was to say, last night."

"Last night wasn't my finest hour."

"Well, this morning isn't mine! At least not until I've brushed my teeth. And stop waving that food at me. Crackers and weak tea are all I can stomach this early in the day."

"So go brush your teeth and I'll make your tea."

"Just stay out of the bathroom," she said, tossing the

warning over her shoulder as she headed down the hall. "I don't need you keeping tabs on how well I floss!"

She didn't bother trying for a complete transformation this time. His opinion of her couldn't sink any lower and it was going to take more than a change of clothes or a touch of lipstick to make him view her more favorably. In any event, he was no oil painting himself right now and so in no position to be critical.

"I've put everything out in here," he said when she showed up in the kitchen. "Your tea's made and I found the crackers. And I must say that if this is your normal diet—"

"It's not," she said shortly. "It just happens to help me get past the morning sickness brought on by the fact that I'm expecting *your* baby."

"Ah, yes, the baby." He snapped the lid off one of the paper cups and helped himself to a pastry. "That's one of the things I want to talk about. I have arrived at a decision."

Her hackles rose at the lordly proclamation. "Well before you award yourself the medal of honor, let me tell you that it isn't going to matter one iota what you've arrived at if I don't happen to agree with it."

He raised his dark level brows in reproof. "Are you always this crabby in the morning, sweet pea, or is it just another manifestation of pregnancy?"

"It's a manifestation of being at my wit's end, if you must know! I'm about ready to burst a blood vessel!"

"Then before you do yourself untold damage, allow me to explain. First, perhaps 'decision' wasn't the best word." He took a bite out of the pastry and munched reflectively. "Perhaps 'solution' will strike a less confrontational note."

"I doubt it, but go on," she said cautiously.

"The way I see things, your family and friends are going to have a feeding frenzy over your latest crisis. They'll be merciless in doling out the pity and advice."

"If this is supposed to make me feel better, it's not working," she said, nibbling at a cracker and wondering how long she could keep it down. "I've already come to the same conclusion and I'd hardly call it comforting."

"So head them off at the pass. Show up with a husband."

This was his idea of a solution? "In case you haven't noticed," she said tartly, "they're a vanishing species where I'm concerned. How do you propose I find one? By running an ad in the newspaper? Or shall I just stand on the street corner and lasso the first likely prospect who happens to pass by?"

He favored her with what he no doubt considered a winning smile. "Neither. You've already got your man. I'm volunteering for the job."

"Don't be ridiculous! You don't even believe the baby's yours."

He polished off the pastry and selected another. "Don't judge me by the way I reacted last night. You caught me unprepared. We were together only that one night, after all."

"One night was obviously enough!"

"Yeah," he said smugly. "We'll have to be more careful in future."

"There is no future," she informed him. "At least not the kind you apparently have in mind. The most I ever wanted from you was an acknowledgment that you're this baby's father. I never asked or expected you to marry me."

"Don't be so hasty in turning me down, Jenna. The idea has definite merit." He took a mouthful of coffee. "The way I see it, we could both do a lot worse."

For a man who, just last night, had as much as told her she was on her own, he was being altogether too agreeable. "Both?" she said suspiciously. "Why, what's in it for you?"

He buried his nose in his coffee cup again and took his sweet time answering. "Let's look at it from your viewpoint first," he suggested, when he came up for air. "First, am I right in assuming you want to keep this baby?"

"Of course I want to keep him! What did you think? That I intended to sell him? I love children! I'd have half a dozen if I could!"

"Calm down, Jenna. I'm just trying to establish where you stand on this, that's all." He tossed his empty cup in the empty bag and helped himself to the one he'd bought for her. "So the big question surely is, wouldn't it be easier for you and better for him if I was part of the equation and living under the same roof?"

He couldn't be serious! "It's always better for a child to have two parents, Edmund, but for us to get married is preposterous. For a start, we aren't in love."

"But we like each other," he pointed out, "and good marriages have been based on much less. In fact, I'd even go so far as to say liking is more essential than being in love. And you can't deny the physical chemistry between us. The sex that night at The Inn was great and at least you know my equipment works the way it's supposed to, which is more than you can say about the last man you almost married."

"That still doesn't explain what you'd get out of the deal."

"I was coming to that. The thing is, you'd be doing me a favor, too. You already know how I feel about Molly, but what you don't know is that ever since the accident, I've been thinking of suing for full custody. The problem is that even if he can prove himself an exemplary father, a single man doesn't stand much of a chance against a stay-at-home mother with a husband in tow. But if you and I were to make application, the odds might well swing in my favor, particularly if I were to produce documented evidence to support my very real concerns for my daughter's well-being.

Bud Horton might be able to keep Adrienne happy where I failed, but he's also the one who backed a tractor over my daughter and damn near killed her. In light of that, I can't see a judge dismissing my claim, can you?''

"You'd go to such lengths just to have Molly living with you?"

"If that's what's necessary to keep her safe." He stretched out his hand and placed it flat against her stomach. "Wouldn't you do the same if someone threatened the baby you're carrying?"

She closed her eyes. "I'd give my life, if I had to."

"There's your answer then. So what do you say? Shall I go out and buy a licence and we'll make it a *fait accompli* before you start sticking out a mile in front?"

"No!" she cried. "I need to give this some thought before I make any decisions."

"What's to think about? You get to save face and have two children for the price of one, and I get my daughter back. Seems to me neither of us has anything to lose and plenty to gain."

"What if Molly doesn't like me? What if the courts don't award you custody even though you're married? Where does that leave us?"

"They're risks I'm prepared to take," he said. "Don't forget, I've got more at stake here than just winning custody of Molly. There's another child to think of, too."

"Does that mean you now accept that you're my baby's father?"

He shook his head ruefully and covered her hand with his. "I accepted that right away, sweet pea," he said. "I just didn't want to admit it. I told you once before, your face is an open book and the truth is there for anyone to read. Pigs would fly before you'd lie about something this important. So, do we have a deal?"

Well, why not? It might not be a marriage made in heaven, but nor would it be made in hell. And truth to tell, the prospect of being Edmund Delaney's wife caused a strange thrill to course through her blood.

Still, instinct urged her to be cautious. "Perhaps," she said. "But let's try being engaged first and see how that works. I want to get to know Molly and make sure she'll accept me, and you ought to meet my family before you become legally tied to me. They won't make the easiest in-laws."

"Okay. If that's the way you want to play it, I guess we can afford to wait a bit longer. But I'm warning you now, Jenna, once I make up my mind about something, I don't change it easily. And from where I stand, there's no doubt this is the best solution for everyone involved, especially the children."

The children. In the end, everything came back to them.

Edmund left about half past eight with the promise that he'd be back around six that evening, and the minute the door closed behind him, the doubts descended and the tug-of-war began.

In terms of time together, they'd known each other less than a week. They were crazy to think they could base a marriage on such short acquaintance. It was almost indecent!

You conceived his baby when you'd known him less than two days. Where was your sense of decency then?

They weren't in love.

They were doing this for the children.

He was using her as a means to gain custody of Molly.

Wouldn't she do the same, if the situation were reversed?

Oh, yes! He'd scored a fatal shot when he'd asked her how she'd feel if she thought her baby was in danger. She knew without a doubt that she'd go to any lengths to protect her child.

Then stop looking a gift horse in the mouth! You've made the commitment, now live up to it!

A long nap, a hot bath, and a visit to a beauty salon to get her hair done went a long way toward boosting her belief that she was doing the right thing. The flower arrangement from Edmund—stargazer lilies and roses—delivered just after she returned to her apartment, didn't hurt, either.

If they both tried, they could make this work. They *had* to. For the sake of the children.

She dressed in a pale green linen skirt and jacket, wore pearls around her neck and matching studs in her ears, and was ready when he knocked on her door again right on the dot of six.

"My, my!" he drawled, eyeing her up and down. "Is it safe to assume, from the way you're all gussied up, that the engagement's still on?"

"It is, unless you've got cold feet."

"Not a chance, Jenna. I already warned you, once I make up my mind, I stick with it. Which is why," he said, producing a gold foil bag from his pocket and dangling it before her eyes, "I've been shopping. Are you going to ask me in, or do I have to drop down on one knee out here and beg you to accept my ring?"

"Ring?"

"To replace the one given to you by the unlamented rooster."

"Oh!" She pulled the door wide and ushered him inside. "Come in, of course. But a ring? You didn't have to go that far!"

"Why not?"

"Because it's not necessary, given the circumstances."

"I don't follow your reasoning," he said, taking a seat

next to her on the couch in her living room. "The circumstances are that you and I plan to get married very soon. It's customary in such instances for the groom to give the bride a ring. You accepted Armstrong's, so why not mine?"

"Because what you and I are planning isn't…the same."

"If, by that, you mean I won't back out at the last minute, then you're right. It isn't the same."

"But it isn't *real.*"

"It's real all right! As real as this." And tipping the bag onto the coffee table, he let a velvet jeweler's box roll out. "There," he said, snapping open the lid so that she could view the contents. "What do you think of that?"

A solitaire diamond of exquisite color and cut set in platinum and yellow gold winked up at her.

"What do I think?" She pressed a hand to her throat in shock. "I think you're out of your mind! This is far too extravagant. I'll feel like a fraud wearing it."

"Get over that idea and fast," he said evenly. "There's nothing fraudulent about this marriage, Jenna, and I expect you to wear my ring as proof." He took it from the box and dropped it into her hand. "Put it on and let's see if it fits."

It did, so well that it might have been custom designed expressly for her. Everything about it was exquisitely perfect.

"You shouldn't have spent so much money," she said, awed and bewildered by his generosity.

"It was affordable," he said brusquely. "Don't make a big deal out of nothing. If you like it, I'll have a wedding band made to go with it."

"Oh, I like it. I like it very much! What woman wouldn't?"

"Then it's settled. Now let's get down to business. First off, have you seen a doctor?"

"A week ago last Wednesday," she said, wishing he

wouldn't keep staring at her midriff as if he expected the baby to pop its head out and say hello. "I'm healthy and she doesn't anticipate any problems. The baby's due sometime between the end of January and the beginning of February."

"Okay. Next item—we need to find a place to live." He cast a glance around the room. "This is a beautiful apartment but it's not designed for children. We'll have to look for a house. Any particular area you fancy?"

"I haven't given the matter any thought."

"What about style? Old? New? Rancher? Two story?"

"Edmund, I don't know! And I think you're rushing things too much. We aren't even sure this arrangement's going to work out."

"It'll work out," he informed her flatly. "I won't have it any other way. What about a wedding date?" He inspected her waistline again. "How long before you start bulging?"

"I don't know. In case you weren't aware, I've never done this before."

"Don't pout, Jenna," he said. "It doesn't suit you."

"Then stop pushing me so hard!"

"It's for your own good."

"How do you figure that?"

"We're engaged," he said patiently, as if she were none too bright. "Engaged couples discuss these things. When people hear about us, they'll ask us what our plans are and they'll expect answers."

"Well, I think getting to know each other a bit more should take precedence. I still couldn't tell people much about you, if they were to ask."

"Sure you could," he said, a wicked, indecent gleam in his eye. "You could tell them I'm a real pistol in the sack and that we make beautiful music together."

She opened her mouth to reply, then snapped it closed

again as the intercom buzzed announcing she had another visitor waiting to be let into the building's main door. Flinging him a repressive glare, she went to answer.

A moment later, she came back to where he sprawled on the couch as if he owned the place. "You might want to think of some other reason I find you so fascinating," she said faintly. "That was my mother. She's on her way up."

CHAPTER SIX

JENNA looked about ready to bolt—headfirst off the balcony, if necessary. "So what's the big deal?" he said. "From the look on your face, anyone would think we'd been caught romping naked in the street."

"You haven't met my mother!" More rattled than he'd ever seen her, she flitted around the room, whisking the jeweler's bag and box into a desk drawer, fluffing the cushions he'd disturbed, repositioning the flowers he'd sent so that the vase sat exactly in the middle of the coffee table.

"You haven't met mine, either," he said, "but I can promise you that when you do, I won't start running in ever diminishing circles and foaming at the mouth. Calm down, for Pete's sake! She can't be *that* bad."

She was that bad and worse! Bleached, permed, thin as a rail, and doing her best to pass herself off as closer to forty than sixty, she breezed into the apartment on a wave of perfume that just about knocked him over. "Your father and I are having dinner downtown and thought we'd get you to join us. He couldn't find parking so he's waiting in the car," she chirped fruitily, then skidded to a halt when she clapped eyes on him. "Good gracious, it never occurred to me you'd be *entertaining*, Jenna. I trust I haven't come at an inconvenient time?"

Both her tone and expression suggested she'd walked in on something too bawdy to bear the light of day.

"Well," Jenna said, looking as if she was going to throw up again any second, "as a matter of fact, Mother, Edmund and I were in the middle of something."

"Edmund?" Eyebrows plucked into near extinction shot up to meet fluffy blond bangs. Pale blue eyes skewered him.

"Edmund Delaney." Jenna waved a distracted hand in introduction. "This is my mother, Valerie Sinclair, Edmund."

He moved a little closer to Jenna and stroked her back reassuringly. "Nice to meet you, Mrs. Sinclair. I've heard a lot about you." Which was a lie, but who was counting!

"It's more than I can say of you," she replied frostily, nostrils pinched with displeasure at the familiar way he was pawing her firstborn. "I've never heard Jenna mention your name."

Jenna's insides gave an ominous gurgle. "That's because Edmund and I...haven't...um..."

She petered into silence and flung him a beseeching look.

"Broadcast our relationship," he finished for her, pasting on his most obsequious smile. "We wanted to keep it just between the two of us a bit longer, but now that you've caught us, I guess we might as well go public. We were discussing wedding plans. Jenna just agreed to marry me."

Valerie Sinclair spared him a glance which, though brief, conveyed her opinion that he needed a lobotomy in the worst way, then fixed Jenna in a beady-eyed stare. "What's he talking about?"

"I'd have thought it was plain enough, Mother," she said, groping for his hand. "Edmund and I are engaged."

"I see. And where does that leave Mark?"

"Nowhere," Jenna said firmly. "I've tried telling you that for weeks, Mother, and you refused to believe me." She thrust out her left hand to show off the diamond. "Maybe this will convince you otherwise and prove that I, at least, have moved on to better things."

"Well! I...hardly know what to say!"

"Congratulations would be nice," Edmund suggested.

"No doubt," Valerie replied, giving her nostrils another

workout. "But you'll have to forgive me if I'm not quite up to par on social niceties, Mr. Delaney. This is a decided shock. We had no idea Jenna was seeing…someone, let alone getting serious about him. Well!" She shrugged her skinny shoulders helplessly. "I suppose you'd better join us for dinner, too. Once he hears the news, my husband will certainly insist on meeting the person who's swept Jenna off her feet in such a mysteriously short time."

"I guess we can accommodate you, just this once," he said, ignoring Jenna's smothered gasp of dismay. "Where are you dining?"

"At The Pavilion."

He should have guessed. Securing a table at one of the city's most exclusive restaurants would be right up Valerie Sinclair's alley! She'd probably lose her appetite for a month if she knew he had a standing reservation there any time he wanted one.

"In case you have trouble finding it," she went on, "it's down on—"

"I know where it is," he said. "Go ahead and don't worry about us. We'll meet you there."

"We can't have dinner with them!" Jenna cried, the minute the door had shut behind the old harridan. "They'll see through us in a flash!"

"They'll see exactly what we want them to see and not a thing more," he told her. "Your mother might like to think she can rearrange the weather to suit her, but she's met her match in me."

"You don't know what you're letting yourself in for, Edmund!"

"I know this is something we have to face sooner, rather than later. We're working to a pretty tight schedule here, Jenna, and while I agree it would have been better if we'd had a bit more time to rehearse, we can't postpone the show indefinitely."

"I can't go through with it!" she moaned, flopping down on the couch like a rag doll. "Not tonight! Not this soon!"

"Sure you can. Just follow my lead. And if things get too dicey, go powder your nose and leave me to handle everything."

"What if you can't?"

He hunkered down in front of her and took her hands. "Hey," he said, "this is me, remember? When have I ever let you down?"

He never had, nor did he that night, and if Jenna wasn't just a little bit in love with him before then, she was afterward.

Her parents were already at their table when she and Edmund arrived and it was clear that her father had heard the news. But he, at least, made an attempt to be gracious.

"So," he said, once introductions were out of the way, "the pair of you plan to get married. I guess that calls for champagne."

"I think it calls for an explanation," her mother said tartly, "because I frankly don't understand how it happened. You're aware, I'm sure, Mr. Delaney, that until very recently, Jenna was engaged to marry someone else?"

Edmund inched his chair closer to Jenna's and smiled at her as if she were the only woman in the world worth a second glance. "Certainly. Jenna and I have no secrets between us."

"Then you must also be aware that we were all quite devastated when things didn't work out as we expected."

"Perhaps you were more devastated than Jenna," he suggested, cutting her off at the pass. "Or else her recuperative powers are greater than yours."

Her mother turned faintly purple while her father, Jenna noticed, disappeared rather hurriedly behind the wine list.

"In any event," Edmund went on, seeming blithely indifferent to the effect his words were having, "she's engaged to me now, so the past is no longer relevant."

"But she can't have known you for more than a few weeks!"

"I'm not one to let the grass grow under my feet, Mrs. Sinclair. I know a good thing when I see it and Jenna is the best thing that's happened to me in a very long time. Neither of us just fell out of the cradle, as I'm sure you'll be the first to admit. We're well past the age of consent and," he finished pointedly, "fully capable of deciding for ourselves how and with whom we wish to spend the rest of our lives."

Mercifully, the waiter showed up then, and after they'd ordered, everyone made a strained attempt to steer the conversation into more a general vein. But the minute their meals arrived and they were unlikely to be disturbed again, her mother picked up right where she'd left off, determined as a bloodhound on the scent.

"You'll have to forgive me if I seem less than delighted by your news, Mr. Delaney, but I'm frankly having trouble coming to terms with the idea of accepting a total stranger as a son-in-law."

"Mother, please!" Embarrassed as much by her own cowardice as her mother's outright incivility, and furious that her father made no attempt to mitigate his wife's remarks, Jenna sprang to Edmund's defense. "I won't tolerate your insulting the man I'm going to marry! If you can't be happy for us, at least have the good manners to keep quiet. And if you can't do that, then—"

Appearing totally undisturbed, Edmund threaded his fingers through hers. "Relax, sweet pea, and try to enjoy your dinner. Your mother's concerned that you're entering a pact with the devil, that's all. Isn't that right, Mrs. Sinclair?"

"I wouldn't go quite that far, but—"

"But you'd find it a whole lot easier to welcome me into the bosom of the family if I were someone you could brag about to your friends. In other words, you'd like to scrutinize my credentials.''

''Well…!'' For once at a loss, her mother dribbled into embarrassed silence and poked around at the food on her plate.

''Then let me put your mind at rest. I'm thirty-five, have a clean bill of health, pay off all my credit cards every month, own a condominium near Lost Lagoon, and run my own business. I make a respectable living and can well afford to support Jenna in some style. I'm an only child. My mother is a happy homemaker. My father is retired and plays golf whenever he gets the chance. I have a university education and have traveled extensively. I am committed to Jenna and to our marriage. I intend to make her very happy.''

Any trace of amusement long since dead, he rested his knife and fork on his plate and leaned forward to spear her mother with a laser-sharp glance. ''Is there anything I've left out?''

''Well…yes,'' she said, dabbing her mouth with her serviette. ''You omitted to mention the kind of business you run.''

He lolled back in his chair again, the smile on his face reminiscent of an alligator moving in for the kill. ''You'll find me in the Yellow Pages under Used Building Materials,'' he said, lifting his wineglass in a mocking toast. ''EJB Limited at your service, madam, with four outlets throughout the lower mainland dedicated to meeting your renovation needs. Perhaps I should mention, though, that my father actually began the business with just one. Unfortunately, he ran into serious financial problems and very nearly had to close down the entire operation, but I was able to turn things around to where things stand today.''

After that revelation, there was no redeeming the evening.

Jenna thought her mother was going to faint dead away, and could well imagine the fallout her father would suffer later.

Used building materials? The man's little more than a garbage collector, Warren! Our future son-in-law makes his living out of a Dumpster and his father probably filed for bankruptcy! How will we ever lift our heads in public again?

Caught between hysteria and nausea, and not sure she could control either, Jenna muttered something about a headache and hurried to the ladies' room for the fifth time in the last hour. When she came out, Edmund was waiting for her near the front door.

"I made our excuses," he said, taking her elbow and towing her out to where his car waited with the engine running. "I don't think they minded too much that we didn't stick around for dessert."

Once in the car, she fairly collapsed from the strain. "I don't know how we lasted as long as we did!"

"Nor I," he remarked dryly. "The next time someone offers you alcohol, sweet pea, try saying 'no' instead of swilling your glass into mine when you think no one's looking. I'd have been pie-eyed if we'd stayed there much longer."

"If I'd refused champagne to toast our engagement, they'd have been really suspicious."

He spared her a quick glance as he shifted into gear and headed south through Stanley Park. "They're suspicious anyway. You didn't eat enough to keep a sparrow alive, you kept disappearing into the ladies' room, and you were so uptight, you could barely string three words together without babbling. If your mother were any more suspicious, she'd try to have me arrested."

The edge in his voice had Jenna covertly studying him, but all she could discern was the rather severe cast of his profile. "I did try to warn you, Edmund."

"You did."

Although the sun had long since set, the night was warm enough that he'd left the top down on the car, but she felt cold suddenly and it took real effort for her to pose her next question. "Are you having second thoughts...about us?"

They were passing the beach by then and instead of answering her, he braked to a stop in a deserted parking area, turned off the engine, and stared out across the bay.

"Edmund?" Heart fluttering with unaccountable anxiety, she said again, "*Are* you having second thoughts?"

"Yes."

"Oh," she said, so dismayed that she almost whimpered.

He turned in his seat and slid his hand around her neck. "Face it, Jenna," he said, his fingers weaving sultry circles on the skin just below her ear, "you don't need the kind of stress you were subjected to tonight. It wouldn't be good for you at the best of times. In your present condition, it's preposterous and I won't allow it to happen again."

"So what do you want to do," she whispered, stunned at the devastation sweeping through her. "End things between us?"

His fingers stilled. "Is that what you think I'm saying?" he asked incredulously.

"Aren't you?"

"Hell, no!"

"You wouldn't be the first man to back out," she said miserably. "And I could hardly blame you if you decided that's what you wanted to do. Tonight was a complete disaster and I don't see it getting any better, at least not where my mother's concerned."

He swore softly and cupped her face between both his hands. "I'm no Mark Armstrong, Jenna," he said, "and I'm not looking for an easy way out of what I admit is a tough situation. Just the opposite, in fact. I vote we make this the shortest engagement on record and set a wedding date, because the sooner you and I are married, the sooner we can stop pussyfooting around other people and get on with our lives the best way we know how."

"But what about Molly? You can't just spring a step-mother on her without warning."

"We'll drive up there on Friday and spend the weekend with her. That'll give you time to get acquainted before we break the news. And remember, she's only four. She isn't going to go looking for hidden motives or ask questions you won't know how to answer." He dipped his head closer to hers. So close that his breath fanned warmly over her mouth. His hand strayed down her shoulder and came to rest mid-way between her waist and thighs, just about where the baby lay snug and safe in her womb. "So what do you say to us making it official the week after next?"

The heat from his hand was creating an urgency in her blood, a flooding awareness between her legs. She wanted to feel him touching her bare skin. He made her ache and quiver. He made her yearn for him so badly that she hardly knew how to contain herself. "I'm not sure I can organize a wedding quite that soon," she said breathlessly.

"Then how does this strike you?" He inched closer. "Let's forget a wedding and just elope. There won't be nearly as many sharks circling if we go that route."

No family, no friends, no guests to speculate on the whys and hows? No witnesses in the event of last-minute hitches?

"Yes," she murmured, her eyes falling closed in antici-pation of the kiss she was sure would soon follow. "Come to think of it, I've had my fill of orchestrated weddings."

"Good!" He planted a swift peck at the corner of her mouth, straightened in his seat and reached for the ignition key.

She almost cried out loud in disappointment. They were engaged. They would be married soon. She was expecting his baby. But he hadn't really touched her since the night she'd conceived and one brief kiss wasn't nearly enough to satisfy her now, not after the evening just passed. "Do you think," she said in a small voice, "that you could kiss me again before we go, and make it last a bit longer this time?"

Very slowly, he shifted back into Park and turned to face her again. "Oh, honey," he said hoarsely, tracing a line from her eyebrow to her jaw and running his thumb over her lower lip, "I can do a lot better than that. All you ever had to do was ask."

He lifted her hand and pressed his lips to her palm. Drew a circle there with the tip of his tongue, a tiny movement so intensely erotic that a jolt of electricity shot to the soles of her feet and left her gasping.

He raised his head. His eyes were luminous in the glow from the dashboard, and full of fire. They scorched over her face, slid the length of her neck to her breasts, then returned to settle on her mouth with searing deliberation.

Blindly, she reached for him, tangling her fingers in his hair. A need unlike any she'd ever known before consumed her. It rose up in her throat, clamoring to be heard. She wanted to tell him things which didn't make any sense. Impossible things, like "I love you!" Impossible because they'd agreed love had nothing to do with their arrangement.

Quickly, before impulse gained the upper hand and ruined the moment, she lifted her lips to his. The faint light from the stars faded to black. The whisper of sea on sand dwindled into oblivion. The entire world retreated until there was nothing but her heart beating next to his, and his mouth closing over hers to weave a spell which promised untold magic in the years to come.

"To think," she said dreamily, many long, delicious moments later, with the taste of him still on her tongue and the scent of him filling her senses, "that a person's life can change so dramatically in such a short time. Not long ago, my future looked so bleak I didn't know how I was going to face it. Then I discovered I was pregnant—something I'd never expected would happen. And soon I'll be married to you, a man I barely know. The whole scenario lacks credibility. Yet when I'm with you, nothing seems impossible. You make me believe in miracles.''

"There aren't any miracles," he said, pulling away from her with flattering reluctance, "just ordinary people doing the best they can with the hand fate deals out to them. Sometimes, things fall into place of their own accord, and sometimes you have to shove the pieces where they belong.''

"Which are we facing?''

"A lot of shoving," he said, "which is why I'm going to drive you home now and leave you at your front door, even though I'd rather be taking you to bed. You've been under a lot of strain lately and it's beginning to show.''

The next week sped by, so crammed with things to do that Jenna had no choice but to leave the running of the day-care center to Irene and two part-time assistants.

"We need to find a house away from downtown,'' Edmund insisted, the day after the dinner debacle with her parents. "Neither your place nor mine has room for a child.''

"But the baby isn't due for another six months," Jenna said.

"I'm thinking of Molly. I can hardly make a case for having her live with us if we don't even have a bedroom for her.''

For three days, they shopped exhaustively, and pored over their shortlist each evening. By the Wednesday, they'd settled on an acre property tucked at the end of a quiet cul de sac in South Surrey, with a view of the ocean and a swimming pool. As an added bonus, there was also a playhouse sure to keep a little girl and her dolls happily entertained when the weather was fine.

On the Thursday, Edmund hired a crew to paint the house, a lovely sprawling rancher with four bedrooms, four bathrooms, a games room, self-contained nanny's quarters above the triple garage, and enough special features that Jenna worried out loud, "Can we afford all this?"

Edmund looked up from the landscape catalog he'd been studying, a smile lurking in his eyes. "Your mother might have me pegged as nothing more than a guy who ekes out a living recycling other people's junk, but I thought you'd have figured out by now that I amount to more than that."

"I haven't drawn any conclusions," she told him. "You said you were gainfully employed and I took your word on it."

"You mean, it wouldn't bother you if I spent my days grubbing around in overalls and wading hip deep in demolition sites?"

"I almost married the heir apparent to a financial empire and look where it got me, Edmund. He might have worn custom-tailored suits and had money to burn, but when it came down to the crunch, I couldn't count on him. So, no, it wouldn't bother me one bit how you dress for work, as long as you're doing what you want to do, and as long as I know you'll be there when I need you, just as I will be for you."

He looked at her thoughtfully for a minute, then dropped the catalog on the table and fished his car keys out of his pocket. "We've got an appointment in an hour with a friend of mine who imports carpets, but let's leave early. There's something I want to show you, first."

He took her to a section of Main Street lined with smart antique establishments, and parked outside a shop with a discreet *EJD Limited* sign engraved on a brass plate above the door.

"*Yours?*" she said, astonished.

"Mine," he replied, ushering her inside.

She might well have stepped back in time to another era.

Floored in foot-wide boards of ancient fir worn to smoothness by the passing of many feet, steeped in the rich smell of fine wood paneling, lit by a hundred or more light fixtures ranging in size from miniature art deco wall sconces to nineteenth century chandeliers large enough to grace a Victorian mansion, the cavernous interior was a virtual treasure trove of architectural collectors' items.

Ornate moldings, carved mantels, intricate wrought-iron railings, beveled glass doors with crystal knobs and fancy brass hinges; finials, spindles, bannisters, and jewel-toned stained glass windows—the variety and quality of goods were a feast for the eyes.

"So this is what you call your Used Building Supplies' business?" She stared around, wide-eyed. "Good grief, Edmund, it's like walking into a museum!"

"As I told your mother, it's just one of four outlets," he said offhandedly. "I have another shop on the North Shore much like this, and two warehouses for storing bigger items, but here is where my father started out and where I spend most of my working day. There's a loft upstairs that's been converted into office space, with a central computer station to track our inventory and keep us up to speed on what's coming onto the market. When I first took over the business, I did most of my buying on-site, which kept me pretty much limited to the immediate area. But now with Internet access, I can bid on items anywhere in the world."

"What can I say? I'm...stunned."

"Don't be," he said. "I didn't bring you here to impress you, just to let you see for yourself that meeting expenses isn't going to be problem. I might not be as filthy rich as the Armstrongs, but I'm not exactly hurting for cash, either."

"I don't care how much money you have, Edmund. That's not why I'm marrying you."

"I know," he said, dazzling her with another one of those

smiles that almost reduced her limbs to water. "That's why I don't mind telling you how much I'm worth. Come and meet some of my staff. They're just about wetting themselves wondering who you are."

"What are you going to tell them?"

"That you're my pet Chihuahua, of course!" He grazed his knuckles up her jaw, and smoothed a strand of hair off her cheek. "You're my fiancée, Jenna, and in another week, you'll be my wife. What do you *think* I'm going to tell them?"

"Aren't they going to be…well…surprised?"

"Probably. But they'll handle it a whole lot better than Mother Sinclair did."

In fact, the two men and one woman in charge of sales took the news completely in stride, probably because Edmund relayed it so casually that it never occurred to them that there might be something strangely sudden about the whole affair.

"I'd say that went pretty smoothly, wouldn't you?" he teased her, when they were back in the car. "No one had a stroke or threw a fit. I'd even go so far as to say they were quite delighted to meet you."

True enough. But as the weekend grew closer, the big question for Jenna was, would Molly feel the same way? Or would she resent the new woman in her father's life? And if she did, what would Edmund's reaction be? Would he have second thoughts about the marriage?

"Go prepared," Irene advised her. "Four-year-olds are easy to bribe! Buy a bunch of little treats that you can dole out one at a time."

"Children aren't that easily fooled."

"And you're not some wicked witch swooping in on your broomstick! Come on, Jenna, you're no novice at handling small children. Quit worrying about making a good impression and just treat her the way you would any of the kids we look after here."

"You might be right."

"I'm *always* right! Now let's talk about what you're going to wear at the wedding."

"Nothing special," she said. "You and one other witness are the only people who'll be there."

"So? You don't dress to please a crowd, my dear, you dress to knock the socks off your bridegroom!"

But even a shopping spree and what Irene described as a two-woman wedding shower and bridal lunch couldn't stop Jenna from vacillating between hope and despair over the coming weekend.

She barely slept on Thursday night. It seemed prophetic when, after nearly three weeks of ideal weather, Friday dawned gray and gloomy, with rain dripping off the trees and the North Shore mountains swathed in mist. By the time Edmund picked her up after work that afternoon, her niggling doubts had ballooned into outright foreboding about what the next two days held in store.

CHAPTER SEVEN

HE GOT to the day-care center just after five. Jenna and another woman stood chatting in the shelter of the front porch, and keeping their eyes on a couple of kids about Molly's age who were having a blast splashing around in puddles on the fenced playground at the side of the building.

Jenna looked a bit wan, he thought. More tired and drawn than a woman in her condition should be. A weekend away would do her good.

"Hi," she said, a tight, nervous little smile flickering over her mouth as he approached. "Can you believe this weather? Oh, this is Irene, by the way. She's my partner here."

Irene weighed about forty pounds more than Jenna, was two inches shorter, and had the kind of placid, capable look associated with people who didn't get easily bent out of shape over insignificant trifles. "Nice to meet you, Edmund," she said pleasantly. "Take this woman away and make her get some rest. She's pushing herself too hard."

"Irene's obviously very fond of you," he remarked, after he'd stowed the luggage and they were on their way.

"The feeling's mutual," Jenna said. "We go back a long way. We've been friends since we both wound up in the same grade nine Home Ec. class."

He tried drawing her out further, asking what had made them decide on the idea of setting up a place where working mothers could leave their preschoolers, why they'd chosen that particular location, and how many children were registered. But her brief answers made it clear she wasn't interested in talking, not about her work or anything else.

That was fine by him. What with the weather, the weekend traffic heading out of the city and clogging the freeway, and the usual quota of insane drivers with a death wish cutting in and out the lanes to gain a three-foot advantage over the guy in front of them, he was better off concentrating on the road.

But when they'd passed Chilliwack and were headed for Hope with most of the commuter congestion left behind, and she did nothing but worry the ring on her finger, he decided the silent treatment had gone on long enough. If he'd done something to tick her off, he'd just as soon she aired it and have done with. "You feeling okay, sweet pea?" he asked warily.

From the corner of his eye he caught her barely perceptible shrug. "Fine."

Stonewalled on that front, he tried another approach. "It takes a good five or six hours to get to Osoyoos and I usually stop for dinner midway, but if you want to eat earlier, just say the word."

"I'm not hungry. Whatever you want is fine with me."

He might have believed her if she hadn't followed up by shifting in her seat as if she wanted to get as far away from him as possible, and staring out the side window.

Ho-hum! A man didn't need a degree in psychology to figure out that something was definitely up. "Okay, out with it," he said. "What's bothering you?"

Silence again, lasting nearly a minute. And only the back of her head facing him, so he couldn't read her expression. Finally, she said, "Have you told your ex-wife about me?"

"Not yet. We aren't usually in touch between visits, unless something comes up with Molly."

"So she has no idea that you're planning to remarry?"

"None."

"How do you think she'll take the news?"

"In her stride." He flicked a curious glance at her, but she was still looking out of the side window. "Is *that* what's got you strung tight as a bow? You think she's going to be upset?"

Slowly, she turned to look at him, her eyes so big and solemn they practically filled her face. "I don't know. That's why I'm asking you."

She'd flung her raincoat in the back seat and was wearing a short red skirt that left an inch of bare thigh showing. He took one hand off the wheel and reached across the console to stroke her knee.

Big mistake! Her skin was cool and smooth as cream, tempting him to explore a little further. His thoughts leaped ahead to the coming night—and other parts, less connected to his brain, just leaped!

"Honey," he said, reluctantly removing his hand before he wound up driving off the road, "if you're laboring under the impression that there's still a lingering attraction between Adrienne and me, put your mind at rest. We don't hate each other, we try to get along for Molly's sake, and we'll always share a connection because of her, but believe me, that's as far as it goes. We've both moved on. She and Bud have been happily married for over a year. Until recently I was just as happily unattached. But now I'm with you."

"Have you ever shown up before with...someone else?"

"Someone else?" He grinned. "You mean a *woman,* Jenna?"

Her cheeks turned all pink. "I shouldn't have asked. It's none of my business."

"Why not? Better to ask than sit and stew about it. And we've already established we've got a lot of history to catch up on. So here's another item for you to file away—I've never shared my weekend visitation rights with another woman because there hasn't been one who mattered enough that I was willing to take time away from Molly." He reached for her again, but this time did the smart thing and clasped her hand. "Until you."

"What if Adrienne doesn't approve of me?"

"Well, first of all, there's no reason for her not to approve of you. And second, who gives a rap anyway? You're marrying me, not moving in with her."

"I guess...." Her sigh turned into a yawn which she tried unsuccessfully to smother. "I'm probably borrowing trouble where it doesn't exist."

"People tend to do that when they're overtired." He squeezed her fingers reassuringly. "You look bushed. Why don't you lower the back of your seat and take a nap before we stop for dinner?"

She must have been more worn-out than even he'd suspected, because she followed his suggestion without another murmur and had drifted off within minutes. He slipped his favorite Louis Armstrong CD into the player, turned the volume down low, and settled himself more comfortably behind the wheel.

The Hope Princeton Highway snaked ahead, wild and deserted. Daylight had died early, shut out by the lowering clouds. Mist swirled in the headlights. The windshield wipers slapped furiously at the rain streaming across the glass. Not a good evening to be driving anywhere, let alone along a stretch of highway as treacherous as this. Chances were, though, conditions would improve dramatically further east.

He glanced down as Jenna stirred and sighed softly in her sleep. Gloom blurred her features so that only the delicate line of her eyebrows and the little fan shape of her eyelashes were discernible. Her skirt had ridden up another inch to reveal a sliver of pale slip. Did she like pretty underwear—silks and satins and stuff like that? Jewelry, perfume, chocolate?

Wrenching his attention back to the road, he blew out a breath. They were getting married within the week, and he didn't even know her birthday, let alone what kind of gifts to buy for her. But he knew that she had a tiny mole next to her navel, and that her skin had flushed like a rose when he'd brought her to orgasm, the only night they'd spent together.

And he knew that he wanted to do the same thing again. Very soon, and very badly.

She was in a much happier frame of mind when she woke up, and dinner lasted longer than he'd intended. But by the time they started on the last lap of the journey, he knew her birthday was in April, that she was two years older than her brother Glen, and that Amber, the baby of the family, was a recent high school graduate with aspirations to be a model.

They left the rain behind just west of Princeton and reached Osoyoos shortly before midnight. The sky was clear and the air filled with the dry desert smell of sagebrush as they cruised down the main street of town.

He'd booked adjoining rooms at a private hotel on the lakefront, a mile or so south of town. He gave her a few minutes to unpack her bag, then tapped on the connecting door. "You feel like going for a stroll along the beach before turning in, Jenna?"

"At this hour?" she said, poking her head out. "I'd have thought you'd be ready for bed."

Oh, he was ready, all right, more than she could begin to guess! "I need to unwind first. All that driving—" *Not to mention thinking about making love to you again!* "—leaves me pretty wound up, especially with the weather being so lousy earlier on."

"Then I'd love to," she said. "I could use a bit of exercise myself. I must've slept for a good two hours in the car. Give me a minute to change my shoes."

He waited for her on their shared veranda which had steps leading directly down to the beach. "How's your room?" he asked, when she joined him.

"Lovely. Very pretty. There's even a thermos of hot chocolate in the sitting area."

"They're famous for taking good care of their guests," he said, holding her hand to help her down the last steep step to the sand and hoping she wouldn't notice that he didn't let go again. "It's one of the reasons I stay here and because they know I'll have Molly with me, they always leave a basket of goodies for her. She gets a real kick out of the place."

"She stays with you overnight then, when you're here?"

"Well, sure! I see little enough of her as it is, without missing out on rubber ducks in the bathtub and bedtime stories."

He'd no sooner spoken than he wished he'd kept his mouth shut. At the mention of Molly's name, Jenna had pulled her hand away and closed herself off in the same silence she'd worn when they'd first left Vancouver. In no time at all, she was working away at her engagement ring until it was spinning like a Ferris wheel on her finger.

Finally, she slowed her steps, toed at the sand, and stared out across the lake. "I can't help worrying about Molly. What if—?"

He cut her off before she had a chance to get properly started. "Don't!" he said, sliding his arms around her waist and holding her tight. "Tomorrow, we'll worry about the what-ifs, but tonight I want to concentrate on us."

She stood stiff as a board in his arms.

"Honey," he said, softening his tone, "we can't make this marriage work if you keep letting other people come between us."

"But our getting married is all about other people!"

"It's also about us. We're the linchpins in this arrangement, Jenna, and if we don't...*gel* as a couple, we might as well call off the whole thing now, because we won't be doing our baby or Molly any favor by getting married."

She was shrinking in his hold, averting her face as if she was afraid of him. And small wonder, with him mouthing off about the possibility of their not sticking together. Where the hell was his brain?

Right down south of his waist, where it had been for hours!

He drew in a deep breath. "I'm not looking for a way out," he said emphatically, "but you've said yourself, more than once, that we hardly know each other."

"We don't," she whispered.

He stroked his hands up her spine and prayed what he was trying to say would come out sounding right. "Then can we please start doing something about that?"

She lifted her face to his. In the faint light from the stars, he could see the question in her eyes. "How?"

Oh, brother! If she couldn't already tell, he ought to see a doctor! "I remember a night when you asked me to make love to you."

"And I remember that you thought it was a bad idea."

He tilted her chin and said unsteadily, "I was wrong."

"Are you saying you want to…have sex with me again?"

"No. I'm asking you to spend the night with me. I'm asking you to let me hold you. And if it turns out that you…want me as much as you've got to know I want you, then I'm asking you to let me make love to you. And this time, I *will* still be there in the morning."

"I don't know," she said, starlight glimmering in her eyes. "I'm not sure that…physical intimacy is the answer."

"It's a place to start." He smoothed a hand over her hair, traced the curve of her ear. "It worked for us before, when neither of us had any expectations of the other. Why can't it work again now?"

"I'm scared," she whispered unsteadily.

"You don't have to be. You can trust me."

"I thought I could trust Mark, too, and I knew him a lot better than I know you."

"Stop harking back to what happened with Armstrong," he said roughly, hating the self-doubt on her face and in her voice. "Don't let him keep coming back to bite you like this. He's irrelevant to us and to our relationship."

"It's not *him,* it's *me.* I'm afraid to trust my own judgment. I'm worried that we're rushing things too much." She bit her lip fretfully. "I don't want to make another mistake, Edmund."

"We are not a mistake," he said vehemently.

For perhaps five seconds she stared at him, different emotions playing over her features. Then the resistance flowed out of her like water seeping out of a sieve. Slowly, she leaned against him, into him, so that her hips melded with his, and her breasts flattened against his chest, and her thighs nestled snugly against his.

He thought he'd explode.

She let her arms creep around his neck. She lifted her mouth to his. She kissed him. Not with the savage hunger that was tearing him apart, but with a simplicity—an innocence, almost—that he found deeply and dangerously moving.

It was all he could do to control the trembling that threatened him. The hunger changed, deepened. He wanted her still. But he also wanted something more yet, for the life of him, he daren't put a name to it.

Slowly, she ended the kiss and pulled away. "Let's go back," she said, taking his hand. "Let's go to bed. Together."

They left the hotel right after breakfast the next morning, and headed west into the low-lying hills. The land was burned to a pale ocher, the sky a deeper blue than anything the more temperate climate on the coast ever produced.

"It's much hotter than it was yesterday," she said.

He turned to look at her. He was wearing sunglasses which hid his eyes, but his smile, like his gaze, was slow and suggestive. "Oh, yes," he said.

Her stomach rolled over. Heat quite unassociated with the soaring temperature outside flamed over her. Last night... long after she'd lain down beside him in his bed...long after he'd kissed her and held her, and promised again that, together, they'd work things out, she'd gone to turn off the bedside lamp.

He'd stopped her, and drawn the strap of her nightgown away from her shoulder and said, "Let me look at you."

She'd shrunk against the pillows, afraid that he'd be repelled by the changes pregnancy had already brought to her body. Her breasts were fuller, heavier, and covered with a tracery of prominent blue veins. But he'd touched them with a wondering fingertip, then with his tongue, and her apprehension had fled, ousted by the lightning streak of pleasure that spiraled through her.

Edmund shifted gears and swung the Navigator along a dusty secondary road. Covertly, she studied his hands on the wheel, strong, square, capable. Able with a single easy motion to make the powerful vehicle do his bidding.

Her gaze slid higher, to his bare forearms, tanned and smoothly muscular. Last night, when she'd been quivering with anticipation and need, he'd supported his weight on those arms and held himself above her, his chest heaving and his eyes heavy-lidded with passion. And when she'd thought she could bear waiting no longer, he'd lowered himself with exquisite restraint and nudged her with the silken tip of his flesh. Teasing her until she was past the point of caring that she was begging him to come into her; pleading with him to assuage the raging ache inside her.

"We're almost there," he said, jerking her attention back

to the present and the challenge confronting her. "This is Bud's land we're passing."

Open country had given way to wire fencing and rows of grapevines neatly staked to supporting trellises. But even though there was no sign of a house or outbuildings, Edmund slowed down and parked in the lee of a slope.

"Why have you stopped?" she asked him, her voice sounding unnaturally high and thin.

"For this," he said, leaning across the console.

His lips swept over her cheek, settled lightly on her eyelids. Turning her head, she found his mouth with hers and clung to him, desperate to preserve the closeness they shared.

His kiss lingered, deepened. Sent flames of hunger curling through her. His fingers touched her face, her neck, tender, featherlight caresses that snatched the breath from her lungs.

"What was that for?" she asked, when her vision cleared and her lungs began working again.

"Just to remind you that we're in this together," he said. "Now smile and look as if you're happy to be wearing my ring, or Adrienne's going to think I had to pay you to wear it."

Soon after, they turned in at a dusty lane. At its end stood a neat little white house with a sloping lawn and a vegetable garden to one side. Behind lay an orchard and beyond that, a cluster of outbuildings.

The Navigator had barely rolled to a stop before the front door of the house opened and a child came hobbling out of the house, her poor little legs pitifully scarred and thin. "Daddy!" she shrieked. "I was watching for you at the window."

"Hey, baby," he said, squatting down and nuzzling her neck. "Have you been waiting long?"

"Very long. For eleventeen hours."

A woman Jenna assumed must be Adrienne appeared, carrying a small suitcase. "It was only about ten minutes, actually," she said, her glance skimming from Edmund and coming to rest on Jenna who'd remained as far in the background as she could get, short of hiding behind the car.

"I've brought you a surprise," Edmund told the child, gesturing for Jenna to join them. "A very special lady. Come and meet her."

The child—*his* child—wound chubby arms firmly around her father's neck and regarded Jenna mistrustfully.

Well, take charge, woman! the other Jenna, the one who handled eighteen preschoolers a day without turning a hair, ordered. *You're the adult here. Don't just stand around looking feebleminded!*

Swallowing, she put one foot in front of the other and came to stand next to Edmund. "Hello, Molly. I'm Jenna."

Molly promptly hid her face in her father's neck and refused to speak another word. "Say hello, baby," he told her softly. "Jenna's going to spend the weekend with us so you can get to know each other."

A muffled "No!" emerged from behind sun-bleached curls and the little thing wriggled out of his arms and attached herself to her mother's leg.

Casting Jenna an apologetic look, Edmund straightened up and said sharply, "Cut it out, Molly! That's no way to behave."

"She's shy," her mother chided him quietly. "And you're not helping matters by speaking to her like that."

"She's not usually shy. I've never known her to act up in front of strangers before. When did all this start?"

Gently extricating her leg from the child's strangling hold, the mother said, "Honey, why don't you go find your new kitten? I bet Daddy and this nice lady would love to meet O'Malley."

Crisis diverted and sunny mood restored, Molly scooted off toward the outbuildings.

Jenna thought the woman handled the situation very well. Edmund clearly did not. "You mean to stand there and tell me you're still letting her run loose in that barn? I thought we had an understanding, Adrienne?"

Rolling her eyes, she said, "She won't be alone. Bud and two of the work hands are cleaning out the hoppers."

"I'm hardly reassured. He was there when a tractor backed up over her, as well. In case it's slipped your mind, he was the one driving it!"

"I'm not getting into this with you again, Edmund, and that's final! What happened was an accident and no one feels worse about it than Bud. As for the way Molly's acting this morning, I'd have thought you were smart enough to figure out that any child who's just spent nearly two months in hospital is going to be very wary of strangers for a while. If you'd let me know ahead of time that you were bringing a guest, I could have prepared her."

Her worst fears come to pass and feeling more of an interloper by the second, Jenna began backing toward the car. She should have waited at the hotel. Better yet, she should have stayed in Vancouver! "I'll leave the two of you to sort this out. It really isn't my business."

She hadn't taken more than three steps before Edmund spoke. "Stay right where you are, Jenna. We're not going anywhere until I've had my say."

"Oh, yes, you are!" Adrienne stepped forward, hand outraised. "If you're determined to go honking on and blow this all out of proportion, Edmund, you'll have to come inside to talk about it where Molly can't overhear. She's gone through enough already, without having to listen to us bickering over her like two dogs with a bone."

It was too late, though. Molly was staggering back down the path from the barn, clutching a scrap of black and white fur in her arms, and squealing for her father to come and look. Flinging an exasperated glare at his ex, he strode off to obey the pint-sized summons.

A small embarrassed silence hung in his wake. Jenna was conscious of the sun blasting over the scene, of the great blue expanse of sky, of heat shimmering over the nearby fields and the drone of honeybees among the flowers bordering the path to the door. And of the woman standing a few feet away.

Tall and pretty, with short blond hair and blue eyes, she was by far the more composed of the two of them. "You've probably guessed I'm Adrienne, Edmund's ex-wife," she said, "and I'm sorry you had to witness that unfortunate exchange. I hope you understand there was nothing personal in the way Molly behaved."

"Oh, please!" Jenna pressed her hands together in distress. "I'm the one who should apologize. I work with children Molly's age and know how easily their security is threatened by strangers. I should never have let Edmund talk me into coming here."

Adrienne grimaced. "But he can be very persuasive. I know. I've been there. When he wants something, there's no stopping him. He just steamrolls over the opposition and flattens it. On the other hand, you must be pretty important to him. This is the first time he's ever shown up with a girlfriend. At least, I assume that's what you are, and not some busybody from children's welfare here to make sure I'm a fit parent to look after a four-year-old."

"Jenna is my fiancée," Edmund said, coming back just in time to hear Adrienne's last remark. "Please don't make her feel any more unwelcome than she already does by suggesting she's here under false pretenses."

"Fiancée?" Adrienne's raised eyebrows spoke volumes. "Well, color me amazed! I had no idea you were even seeing anyone, letting alone seriously involved. Isn't this rather sudden, Edmund?"

There was no malice in her remarks. If anything, she was almost teasing him. Edmund, though, remained on the offensive. "I wasn't aware I was supposed to keep you informed of my plans."

"Oh, shut up and stop being so pompous!" she said cheerfully. "Jenna, please accept my very best wishes. Edmund can be a bit of a handful sometimes as you've probably already found out, and I don't envy you trying to keep him in line, but you could do a lot worse. As for Molly, give her time and she'll come around. She's a pretty easygoing kid as a rule. It's just that she's been through a lot in the last little while."

"Yes, Edmund told me," Jenna said.

"Oh, I'm sure—with bells on, I bet! But regardless of what he's led you to believe, Bud and I aren't a couple of half-wits not fit to be left in charge of a flea, let alone a child."

"I didn't for a minute think you were."

"Well, thanks. Hopefully you can convince him, as well."

They left shortly after, with Molly strapped in the back seat with her favorite teddy bear. She refused to look at Jenna, though. Instead, she hid her face behind the stuffed toy and pursed her little rosebud lips into a disapproving pucker.

"Was that a complete nightmare?" Edmund asked in a low voice, as they drove down the lane in a cloud of dust.

"Not entirely. I liked Adrienne very much. I thought she was genuinely happy for you when you told her about us, and that, at least, was a relief."

"You'll like Molly, too, when you get to know her."

"I'm sure I will." Jenna started twisting her ring, then stopped when she saw that he'd noticed. "It's whether she'll ever take to me that has me worried."

"Don't be. Because Adrienne's right, you know. Kids

Molly's age adjust quickly. She didn't make any fuss about coming with us, once she got over her little fit of the sulks.''

She wasn't over the moon about it, either!

"After lunch, we'll take her in the pool. She'll love it and the specialist told us getting her to exercise her leg in the water is the best thing we can do to help restore her muscle mass."

"Maybe it should be just the two of you," Jenna said. "I don't think we should try to force the issue of me being involved."

"No." He gave the steering wheel a little thump. "We're going to start out the way we intend to carry on, and the sooner she realizes that, the sooner she'll accept you."

Of course, it wasn't nearly that easy. When Jenna joined them on the pool patio, Molly took one look at her and ordered, "You go home."

But Jenna had come prepared and didn't wait for Edmund to wade into the fray. "Okay," she said, digging a pair of butterfly barrettes out of her straw bag and holding them on the palm of her hand. "But will you let me give you these first?"

Suspicion fought a brief and losing battle with guileless four-year-old avarice. "Can I keep them?"

"Sure."

"Can I take them home?"

"Yes."

Molly edged closer. Snatching opportunity the minute it presented itself, Jenna the preschool expert came to the fore. "Want me to show you how to put them in your hair?"

"No," the child said. "I want my daddy to do it."

"Count me out," Edmund said from the sidelines. "I don't know how."

"Tell you what." Jenna put the butterflies on the umbrella table next to their towels. "I'll leave them here and if you decide you want to wear them, you can tell me."

Molly eyed the straw bag. ''Do you have more treats in there?''

''I might have.''

''For me?''

''Maybe. If you'll show me how you can swim.''

''Daddy has to hold me, but,'' she allowed, ''you can watch.''

''That was bribery,'' Edmund muttered in Jenna's ear as he led Molly toward the pool.

''So?''

''So you're smarter than I am.'' His gaze roamed over her suggestively, conjuring up memories of the night before with chaotic effect on her blood pressure. ''And better looking, too.''

After that, things didn't seem quite so bleak, especially when Molly came out of the water, planted her little dimpled elbows on Jenna's lap and said, ''I want those things in my hair now.''

Edmund muttered, ''Remind her to say 'please.' ''

But Jenna wasn't about to blow a heaven-sent opportunity to earn a few Brownie points just for the sake of manners. ''That can come later. Right now, we need to worry about the tangles in these curls.'' She took a wide-toothed comb from her bag. ''Come here, sweetie, and let's get you fixed up.''

Still keeping a suspicious eye on proceedings, the child allowed her to work through the snarls and pin the barrettes in place. ''Am I pretty?'' she asked artlessly, when the job was done.

For the first time that day, Jenna's smile came without effort. ''Oh, yes. Very pretty!''

Molly folded her sweetly rounded arms, so different from her poor withered little legs, and regarded Jenna gravely. ''You're pretty, as well.''

Caught off guard by the rush of emotion which swept over her, Jenna blinked and bit her lip. "Oh, darling, thank you!"

"But not as pretty as Mommy," Molly informed her, just in case she was getting ideas beyond her station.

"Of course not," she said. "No one's as pretty as your mommy."

"I have to disagree," Edmund remarked slyly, draping his towel over the chair next to hers. "I consider my fiancée to be a real tight package."

"Tight package?"

He flopped down beside her and batted his wet eyelashes at her lecherously. "Beautiful, even!"

He had a beautiful mouth, a beautiful voice—a beautiful everything. And she ought to know. Inspired by his passion the night before, she'd responded with a degree of daring which, in retrospect, made her blush. There wasn't an inch of him that she hadn't explored.

"You're not half-bad yourself," she said, glad she was wearing her sunglasses so that she could stare her fill without being too obvious about it.

He linked her fingers in his and swung their joined hands between the chairs. "Everything's going to work out, sweet pea. You're over the worst with Molly. It's going to be a piece of cake from now on."

But Jenna knew better than to take too much for granted. Children needed time to adjust to change, and it would be a mistake to push too hard, too soon.

"You go without me and I'll fend for myself," she insisted, when Edmund suggested an early dinner so that Molly would get to bed at a reasonable hour. "She needs to have some time alone with you, especially this first time. It's important to reassure her that, just because I'm part of the picture now, she hasn't lost her daddy."

She didn't expect to see him again that night. Molly's bedtime rituals weren't something that should be rushed.

And for herself, she wouldn't mind turning in early. Although last night had been wonderful, it hadn't exactly been restful and she assumed Edmund would be as tired as she was. So she was surprised to hear a soft rap at the connecting door just after half past nine.

Concerned there was some problem with Molly, Jenna threw back the sheet and hurried to answer. Stripped to the waist, Edmund stood on the threshold, the light beige of his twilled cotton pants in striking contrast to his deeply tanned skin. As far as she could determine, the child lay sleeping peacefully in one of the beds behind him.

"What is it?" she whispered.

"Do you have to ask?" Leaving the door ajar, he stepped into her room and reached for her.

"No!" Aghast, she backed away. "Edmund, we can't...do *that!*"

"I know," he whispered. "I just came to say good night."

"Good night!" She placed the flat of her hands against his chest and tried to push him away.

But touching him was a bad idea—and standing close enough for him to touch her, even worse. The warmth of his skin, the nearness of his mouth, the way his eyes turned a sultry near-purple in the lamplight, were not conducive to good sense. And his mouth brushing hers...!

"You *have* to leave," she breathed, even as her hands strayed over the firm contours of his ribs. "What if Molly wakes up and sees us?"

"She won't. Once she's asleep, she's gone for the night." His tongue wove a heated trail from her lips to the corner of her jaw, dipped into the whorl of her ear, once... twice...three times, and unleashed such far-flung repercussions that her thighs trembled.

She sagged against him, damp and aching. He slipped his hand inside the deep vee of her nightgown, found her breast, drew it free. His other hand closed over her bottom and pulled her against him, hip to hip. The hard, pulsing strength of him was as unmistakable as the moist response of her own flesh.

This is wrong! her ever-vigilant conscience warned. But the louder voice of passion overrode it. With a soft moan of defeat, she collapsed onto a nearby chair.

He dropped to his knees, lifted her bare foot, kissed her instep, her ankle, her calf. He raised her nightgown and blew a stream of cool air over her thighs and they, poor feckless things, fell slackly apart and willingly betrayed her.

Biting her lips to keep from crying out loud, she knotted her fingers in his hair and swayed toward him, all kinds of absurd, unguarded words—*I love you! I need you!*—clamoring to be heard.

But another voice spoke first. A child's sweet treble fogged with sleep and asking uncertainly, "Why are you doing that to my daddy? Does he have tangles in his hair, too?"

CHAPTER EIGHT

OF COURSE, they both damn near jumped out of their skins. In fact, Jenna was in such a hurry to distance herself from him that she came close to maiming him in his most tender parts.

Flinging on the robe lying over the foot of her bed, she rushed to pick up Molly. "No, darling," she crooned, hiding the kid's face in her neck as if the sight she'd wandered in on might scar her for life. "We were just...just..."

"Just wrestling," he said lightly, aiming to defuse the tension of the moment with a little levity.

The expression on Jenna's face was enough to stop a clock. She was obviously furious—as much with herself as with him. "Don't make matters worse!" she hissed.

"Don't *you* overreact!"

She seared him with a glance. "So much for her never waking up once she's been put to bed! A fat lot you know!"

"She's already asleep again, sweet pea," he said mildly. "You're getting stewed up over nothing. I'll bet you dollars to donuts she won't remember a thing about all this in the morning."

He should have left out the "sweet pea." In fact, he should have kept his mouth shut altogether and she wasted no time telling him so. "Be quiet, you...insensitive clod!"

"Hey, pardon me for finding you desirable!" he said. "And not to put too fine a point on it, but I didn't seem to strike you as too repulsive, either."

She turned away, but not before he saw the blush staining her face. "I'm putting this child to bed, and I want you out of my room by the time I'm done."

"Give her to me. I'll save you the trouble," he said, becoming annoyed himself.

"I can manage," she said snottily. "Thank you."

"She's too heavy for you to be lugging her around in your condition. And she is *my* daughter."

Ah, jeez! Why did he have to go and say a thing like that? She looked crushed. Devastated. And small wonder. "Hey," he said, touching her arm. "Jenna, I'm sorry."

"Don't be. I'm the one who's sorry for overstepping my bounds. Here, take her."

He lifted his sleeping daughter out of her arms. "I'll be back and we'll sort this out," he said. "Just give me a minute to tuck her in."

In fact, it probably took him no more than thirty seconds. Molly was out cold and didn't even move when he laid her in the bed. But thirty seconds was long enough for Jenna to have closed the door between their rooms and he'd have bet money that she'd locked it, too.

They started back to Vancouver midway through the afternoon the next day. Jenna had opted out of going with him when he took Molly home after lunch, but she'd been really sweet with her that morning, producing a bunch of little goodies that she'd got stashed in her bag and generally going out of her way to give Molly a good time.

It had paid off, too. In no time flat, Molly was hanging on to her like a limpet and he might as well not have been there, for all the attention she paid to him. She asked no pointed questions about last night's incident and as he'd expected, clearly didn't remember a thing.

Jenna was a different matter. Though warm and affectionate with his daughter, her refusal to look him in the eye, coupled with her general touch-me-not attitude, made it plain that their relationship had fallen off the stove and into the deep freeze.

He wasn't about to put up with that. "So," he began, once they'd cleared town and were headed back to the coast, "how long are you going to keep this up?"

"I beg your pardon?"

"You heard me, Jenna, and you know damn well what I'm talking about, so spare me the long-suffering po-face and air what's on your mind. I had enough of the silent treatment when I was married to Adrienne. I don't need another round of the same thing from you. If you're still ticked off about last night, say so."

"I'm *embarrassed* about last night," she said. "And ashamed, too, if you must know. I never thought of myself as the kind of person who'd behave so irresponsibly in front of a child."

"Jenna," he said on a sigh, "it was unfortunate that Molly happened to walk in on us when she did, but we weren't doing anything wrong."

"Oh, please! How can you say that?"

"Admittedly, we got carried away and that was mostly my fault. But cripes, it wasn't as if we'd been caught *doing* it!"

She gave a strangled laugh. "Another five minutes and we would have been!"

"So? Face it, Jenna—little kids Molly's age walk in on their parents all the time. Do you plan to put a lock on the bedroom door once we're married, in case we get caught playing leapfrog?"

"For a start, I'm not her parent, I'm a complete stranger. And second, we're not married. And third, how you can *joke* about this is beyond me!"

"I'm trying to put the whole thing in perspective, something you seem unable to do. Look at the big picture—the weekend was a smashing success. You were worried that Adrienne might disapprove of you, that Molly might not accept you, and you came through both tests with flying colors. Shouldn't that count for more than a ten-second episode that only you and I remember?''

''I think we're trying too hard to cram into a few days something which takes months to achieve. Molly might have had fun with me today, but she doesn't know me and she has no reason to trust me. I'm not the one she'll run to if she skins her knees or the one she wants tucking her into bed at night, and I don't think she's ready to accept us as a couple.''

''I don't like where all this talk is leading,'' he said, suspicions on high alert. ''What's the bottom line here, Jenna?''

''I think we're putting too much pressure on her—on all of us. In my opinion, we should postpone getting married.''

He'd been afraid of that. ''No!''

''We're rushing things too much, Edmund.''

''You should have thought of that before you begged me to make love to you at The Inn.''

''I was distraught then.''

''And you're pregnant now, or have you forgotten that?''

''I do believe I almost had,'' she said, sounding surprised. ''It got pushed to the back of my mind with everything else that's happened.''

''Then I suggest you bring it back to center stage. Molly is one of two compelling reasons we decided on marriage in the first place, and that infant you're carrying is the other. Postponing our plans won't benefit either of them.'' He shot her a sideways glance. ''Or does the reason you're getting cold feet have to do with Molly? Have you changed your mind about taking on a stepdaughter?''

''No!'' she exclaimed, doing a number on her ring. ''She's a beautiful child and I don't see how anyone could fail to love her. But I admit I'm not altogether comfortable with the idea of your going after custody. Your concerns all sounded very valid when you first told me about them, but now that I've met Adrienne, I can't help wondering if you're not going to extreme measures over—''

"You want to talk about extreme?" he snapped, livid suddenly. "How about extreme negligence? You saw Molly's legs—and let me tell you, they're a hundred percent improved over the way they were a month ago. You saw how her gait is still affected from her pelvic injury. You saw her being allowed to go back to the very place where she nearly got killed. And when I objected, you heard her mother dismiss me as being overprotective.''

"Oh, Edmund," she said, with more warmth than she'd shown all day, "I *do* understand how worried you are. I know how close you came to losing your little daughter.''

"Then you ought to be able to understand why I'm not waiting until another accident happens before I take steps to ensure her safety.''

"But Adrienne struck me as a sensible, caring woman.''

"You figure you know her better than I do, after no more than ten minutes' conversation with her?''

"I don't think she'd deliberately expose Molly to danger.''

"It happened once and I don't see any steps being taken to prevent it from happening again. You can afford to take the high road, Jenna, because Molly isn't your child and you didn't see the shape she was in, the day of the accident. But I did and I can tell you this—if it had been *your* baby whose life was on the line, and you were left to pace the floor wondering if he was going to make it, you wouldn't be so full of optimistic charity and no measure to protect him would strike you as too extreme.''

She held both hands flat against her belly protectively. "No," she said, ashen-faced. "I don't imagine it would.''

"Then please, don't even think about backing out of our arrangement. Not if you really care about the welfare of our children.''

He couldn't have hit a more sensitive nerve if he'd tried. "Well, of course I care," she said soberly. "The children must always come first. Don't ever doubt that."

"Okay then. So let's not hear any more talk about postponing the wedding."

They were married the following Saturday. Jenna wore the dress she'd bought when she and Irene went shopping, a printed polished cotton affair with a portrait collar and dropped waist which disguised the slight thickening around her middle. Edmund wore a navy blazer and gray trousers.

She walked into the courthouse at noon as Ms. Jenna Sinclair, and walked out again fifteen minutes later as Mrs. Edmund Delaney. The ceremony, witnessed by Irene and Jim Harte, a friend of Edmund's, took all of ten minutes.

Afterward, the four of them went out for lunch in the park. Edmund ordered sparkling apple juice for her and champagne for everyone else. Jim proposed a toast; Irene proposed another. And Jenna behaved the way a bride was supposed to behave, smiling at all the right times and saying all the right things.

But inside, she felt numb, bewildered; a woman caught up in a situation moving at such lightning speed that she'd lost control of it. The week had raced by, one day after the next so filled with appointments that she'd once again been forced to take time off from work. There were rugs to buy for the house; window coverings, new appliances, linens and furniture to be ordered; work crews to instruct, landscape architects to consult.

If she was overwhelmed, though, Edmund was very much on top of things. He'd gone with her for her prenatal checkup on the Monday. "Why not?" he'd reasoned. "These days, fathers don't wait until the baby's born to get involved and with this one I intend to be a hands-on parent from the start."

On Wednesday, he insisted on buying her a new car.

"I don't need a new car," she told him. "I like the one I've got."

He'd dismissed that argument with a flick of his hand. "It's a two-seater and you've already told me it keeps breaking down. You need a more dependable family-oriented vehicle."

"Edmund, the baby's not due for another five and a half months!"

"But Molly's already here, and too young to ride in the front seat."

True. But there were a dozen more pressing issues to deal with just then, and how often would she be driving Molly anywhere in the next little while?

On the Thursday, he sent two of his employees over with a truck to pack up and move to the new house those possessions she was keeping.

"It'll feel more like home if you've got some of your own things around you," he said, when she suggested waiting until things calmed down a bit before worrying about closing up her apartment. "Your happiness—and our children's well-being, of course, are what matter most to me."

When she tried to tell him she didn't need him to organize her every waking moment, that she was used to looking after herself and was more than capable of choosing a length of drapery fabric or a new car without his supervision, he'd put his arms around her and say, "You're pregnant, sweet pea. You can't run around doing everything the same as usual. You need more rest and that's where I come in. We're a couple now, and it's my job to look after you."

How could she tell him that by the very act of rushing everything along at such a pace, he was defeating his stated purpose? She had never felt more harried, or more exhausted.

"Don't take on too much," her doctor warned her.

But the days weren't long enough to get everything done.

Just when she'd had enough of being chivied around and was ready to put her foot down, though, he'd arranged a quiet evening for just the two of them and made stunning, exquisite love to her that smoothed away all her abrasive edges and left her so molten with hunger for him that she could hardly wait to be his wife and lie beside him every night.

Still, it seemed unnatural that she hadn't yet met her husband's family, or that Molly hadn't been told her daddy was remarrying. It lent a sneakiness to the wedding day that Jenna found disturbing, and made their marriage seem less the sensible arrangement they'd intended than a trap set to take the unwary off guard.

"How are we going to let everyone know about us?" she asked him, after they'd said their goodbyes to Irene and Jim, and were driving to their new home.

"We'll have a party tomorrow night and announce the news then."

Assuming he was joking, she said, "Edmund, I hate to have to break it to you, but I can't possibly organize a party in twenty-four hours."

"You don't have to, sweet pea," he said, pinning on his most dazzling smile. "It's already been taken care of."

"Taken care of how?"

He shrugged. "The usual thing. Caterers, bartenders, flowers."

"And what about guests, or are we the only ones who'll show up?" she said, still only half-believing him. "People need advance notice, you know."

"And they got it. Your folks, mine, friends, business acquaintances—they'll be there with bells on. I took the liberty of sending out invitations earlier this week. I thought you deserved something a bit more memorable and lavish to mark your wedding day than lunch for four in a crowded restaurant.''

"You're serious!" she said, too stunned to be angry.

"You bet!"

She swallowed. "Did it never occur to you that I might like to be consulted before you went ahead with this?''

"Honey,'' he said, all injured innocence and sweet male reason, "I didn't want you being run off your feet any more than you already have been. I figured you'd be as eager as I am to spread the word that we're married and it seemed to me that getting everyone together in one place and breaking the news that way was the most efficient route to go.''

"Efficient?'' she said, indignation finally outstripping astonishment. "How about overbearing? I assumed marrying you meant I'd be mistress of my own house, but I'm beginning to feel more like a piece of furniture!''

He covered her knee with his hand and favored her with what he no doubt considered a sultry gaze. "Some piece of furniture!'' he growled.

"Exactly what did the invitations say?'' she demanded, slapping his hand away. "That Edmund Delaney would be putting his new house and wife on display?''

"You do me an injustice, Jenna,'' he said mournfully. "They were simple, straightforward invitations to an open house being held in your honor.''

And just like that, he did it again: made her feel like an ungrateful harpy who didn't have the brains to know when she was well-off!

Edmund's parents were the first to arrive but Jenna barely had time to shake their hands before other guests started pouring through the door, which was a pity. They seemed such a nice, unassuming couple that they surely deserved better than to be lumped in with a host of strangers to hear that their son had taken another wife, and she'd have liked the chance to break the news privately.

But, ''Don't feel you have to keep us company,'' his mother said kindly, obviously not having the foggiest idea of what the evening was really all about. ''Billy and I will be quite fine by ourselves. Edmund hasn't thrown a party like this in years—not since his divorce. We're just so pleased to see he's taking time for a social life again, and it's lovely to be included in such an elegant affair.''

Well, she had a point. Edmund had certainly spared no expense or effort in putting the party together. All Jenna had had to do was spend a leisurely two hours getting dressed and squeezing herself into an outfit which suddenly felt at least two sizes too tight. By the time she was ready, the catering staff had taken over the rest of the house.

There were flowers and candles throughout the reception rooms, little tables on the patio, lights strung through the trees in the garden. Maids in uniform had prepared trays of hot and cold canapés, white-jacketed bartenders stood guard over magnums of champagne chilling in silver buckets, two valets were stationed outside the front door ready to park cars.

Edmund had been waiting for her in the front hall, too handsome for his own good in a charcoal suit, white shirt and oyster-gray tie. ''Well?'' he'd said, tucking her hand under his arm and parading her around to inspect his handiwork. ''Will it do?''

''I can't fault you on a single detail,'' she said, knowing that even if he'd made a complete mess of the whole affair, she'd have forgiven him after the afternoon they'd spent making love. Whatever their differences elsewhere, in bed they were utterly and blissfully compatible. ''Everything's perfect. I couldn't have done half the job, even if I'd had a week to prepare.''

''And you, my dear, are exquisite. Pregnancy suits you.''

"I hope," she said, glancing around nervously, "that you aren't planning to make *that* public knowledge, too!"

He eyed her waistline speculatively. "We can hold off for now, but it's becoming pretty self-evident. You're beginning to show, sweet pea. You'll be in maternity clothes in another week."

The observation didn't do a whole lot for her composure, particularly not with her family showing up en masse before he'd finished speaking.

"Oh dear," she said, clutching his arm a little tighter.

He followed her gaze and muttered, "Oh dear, indeed! I take it the gentleman with the designer haircut is your brother and the petulant young thing bringing up the rear, your sister?"

She almost laughed at his appalled expression. "Right on both counts."

If impressing her parents had been part of his plan, he succeeded in spectacular fashion. "Well, I had no idea!" her mother gushed, returning from a thorough inspection of the premises after they'd gone through the obligatory introductions. "Why didn't you say you were so...?"

"Comfortably situated?" Edmund supplied. "Mrs. Sinclair, I had no idea you cared!"

Maintaining a straight face with difficulty, Jenna said, "Perhaps now's a good time to make the announcement. I can't keep hiding my left hand indefinitely."

"Right." He signaled the bartenders to distribute the champagne and when everyone was served, led her into the middle of the room, raised his glass and said, "Ladies and gentlemen, I'd like to propose a toast. To my lovely wife, Jenna Delaney!"

Feeling rather like a prize heifer in a show ring, Jenna did her best to look slim and composed. The silk jersey dress and matching jacket she wore camouflaged her expanding middle to any but the most observant eye, but finding herself the sole object of everyone's unwavering attention made her feel horribly self-conscious.

"Smile, sweet pea," Edmund murmured in her ear. "You're supposed to look radiant, not hunted."

"I can't help it. My mother's making a beeline for us, with outraged curiosity written all over her face!"

"Leave everything to me." He shot his cuffs and squared his shoulders. "I'll deal with her."

The last guests left around ten-thirty. Jenna had been visibly wilting for at least an hour before that, so he sent her off to bed while the catering staff cleaned up. Once they were done and had driven off, he removed his jacket and tie, poured himself a cognac, turned off all but one of the lights, and went outside.

It had been clear earlier, but clouds had moved in from the west and the atmosphere hung heavy with the sort of stillness which usually signified a summer storm. It couldn't be any worse than the one he'd stirred up that evening, though!

Valerie Sinclair had wasted no time before wading in for the attack. "I cannot believe what I just heard, Jenna! In fact, I'd go so far as to say I find your actions unnaturally secretive."

"'Private' is the word I'd choose," he'd said, angling himself so that Jenna was shielded from the worst of the onslaught. "And that's the way we both wanted it to be."

"Well, I feel cheated! Every mother lives for the day she sees her daughter walk down the aisle on her father's arm. You took away my right to give her the kind of wedding she—"

"Missed out on the last time," the sullen looking other daughter supplied spitefully. "But I guess that's why you wanted to elope, isn't it, Jenna? So that no one would know if the bridegroom took a hike again?"

"Watch your mouth, young lady!" he'd snapped. "I won't tolerate that kind of talk about my wife."

She sniffed and flung back her hair, the gesture so affected that he was pretty sure she'd spent hours practicing in front of a mirror. "Whatever!"

"We chose to get married quietly because a fancy wedding would have been inappropriate, especially coming so soon after May's disaster," Jenna said, trying to smooth things over.

Obviously deciding there wasn't much she could do but accept what she couldn't do anything to change, her mother pasted on a saintly expression. "Well, it's your life and I hope you don't live to regret acting so hastily." She held out a scrawny paw. "Welcome to the family, Edmund."

The brother, Glen, who'd been busily casing the room along with every other part of the house and garden when he wasn't leaning on the bar, shoehorned his way into the conversation. "Mom tells me you run your own business. From the looks of it, you must be doing all right because my sister doesn't have the kind of cash needed to buy and furnish a place like this."

"I get by."

"Pretty handsomely, I'd say." He eyed the rugs, the painting above the fireplace, the sterling candlesticks on the rosewood table—did everything but pick up a plate in his manicured hands and turn it over to see what brand of china they owned. "Jenna's done all right for herself. Maybe we won't miss Mark as much as we thought."

"I work hard for my money," Edmund had replied, having a pretty clear idea where the conversation was leading.

Glen aspires to big things but unfortunately lacks the drive to achieve them himself, Jenna had warned him. *Mark had promised him a position in his company which involved great rewards in return for very little effort, and he's still mourning the lost opportunity.*

That he was actively seeking another sucker to fill the absent Mark's shoes became immediately apparent. "If you need any help," he said, his attempt to sound casual sadly undercut by the avarice gleaming in his eyes, "I'd be glad to give you the benefit of my experience and take some of the load off your shoulders."

"Are you asking me for a job?" Edmund asked him levelly.

"I could make myself available, given the right circumstances."

Tiring of the game and figuring he might as well start out the way he intended to go on, Edmund had put the bombastic little twerp out of his misery. "Fine. Be at my South-East Marine Drive outlet at seven tomorrow."

"In the *morning?*"

"I might be a hard taskmaster, Glen, but I don't expect my people to work nights."

"Well, I guess not! But seven's a bit early to open an office, wouldn't you say?"

"Who said anything about an office? You'll be working in the warehouse, unloading stock and pulling inventory as it's needed. Wear safety boots and jeans. The foreman will issue you coveralls and a hard hat when you get there."

"Warehouse?" Valerie Sinclair screeched, clutching a flabbergasted hand to her bony chest. "Hard hat? Young man, you can't be serious! My Glen doesn't *do* manual labor!"

"Then I guess he'd better look elsewhere for a handout," Edmund advised her shortly, "because that's my best offer. And now, if you'll excuse us, my parents are waiting to meet my bride."

"You wicked thing!" Jenna had exclaimed under her breath as he led her away. "Don't you know you've just dealt poor Glen's ambitions a death blow?"

"Poor Glen needs a boot in the rear! Unfortunately, he doesn't seem inclined to let me administer it."

Thank God Jenna had made a better impression on *his* folks! "We're surprised, of course," his father had said, shaking his hand, "but it's the kind of surprise we can handle. We're delighted for both of you."

His mother had kissed him and gone all misty-eyed. "You have wonderful taste," she whispered. "Jenna's lovely, Edmund. Congratulations and very best wishes to both of you. And please come for dinner soon so that we can get to know our new daughter better."

Too bad his in-laws hadn't seen fit to be as gracious!

Thoughtfully, he sipped his cognac. Funny how much a man's life could take a different turn in the space of a heartbeat. Three months ago, his whole world had threatened to come crashing down with the news of Molly's accident. He'd undergone some of the darkest hours of his life, waiting to hear if she was going to live.

Yet, at unexpected moments during the bleak days that followed, memories of Jenna had slipped into his mind. He'd found himself wondering how she was coping, and wishing he'd had the chance to explain to her why he'd disappeared so abruptly. He'd vowed that if—*when* Molly was out of danger, he'd look up the woman who'd succeeded where others had failed, and touched his heart with her fragility and need. He'd let her know that if she needed a friend, she could count on him.

Had it been because he'd felt so alone in his sorrow for his daughter? Was that what prompted him, when life grew bearable again, to follow up on his promise, and so find himself where he was today?

Marriage, another child…they'd been the last things on his mind when he'd knocked on her door that night, less than four weeks ago. Yet here they were now, and damned if it didn't look to be the smartest move he'd ever made.

With any luck, Molly would be living with them before Christmas. God willing, they'd have a healthy baby in the new year. And tonight, he had a wife waiting in bed for him, and a familiar hunger stirring in his blood.

Not that it was all violins and roses! The party had been a gamble and Jenna had been pretty ticked with him about it, but she'd come around and in the end, it had paid off. They'd crossed another hurdle and launched themselves as a married couple.

Yeah, for a loveless arrangement, things were working out pretty well!

Satisfied, he drained his glass and turned back to the house just as the first distant thunder rolled across the sea.

CHAPTER NINE

AT SEVENTEEN minutes after five the next morning, Jenna awoke to a haunting apprehension that made no sense at all.

Early sunshine flooded the room. A light sea breeze lifted the filmy drapes at the open window and brought the scent of flowers and damp earth into the room. Birdsong filled the air.

Last night, she and Edmund had made love. After, she had fallen asleep in his arms, a happy, fulfilled woman. He sprawled beside her now, his breathing deep and regular.

Everything was wholesomely, reassuringly normal. So what had awakened her so suddenly, and at such an unearthly hour?

Then it came again, a slow deadly cramping in her lower abdomen that advanced and receded like waves creeping up the shore. And even though she'd had no previous experience with pregnancy, she recognized the metallic taste in her mouth as fear, and knew instinctively that her baby was in trouble.

"Edmund!" she whispered, too terrified to move.

He muttered inaudibly and rolled over so that his back was toward her. Inching herself to a sitting position, she shook his shoulder. "Edmund, wake up, please!"

Groaning, he lifted his head, looked at the clock on his side of the bed, and fell back against the pillows. "It's too early to get up," he said, his words slurred with sleep.

And over five months too soon for her to be in labor!

But the cramping, she realized with enormous relief, was easing, and she wondered if she'd panicked for nothing. Maybe she'd just been lying in one position for too long, or she needed to spend a penny. According to all the books, frequent urination was symptomatic of pregnancy, especially first thing in the morning.

Gingerly, she pushed aside the covers, climbed out of bed, and stole into the bathroom. Closing the door, she leaned against it and prayed, making desperate bargains with God to let her be mistaken, to keep her baby safe, no matter what the cost.

On the wall opposite, the mirrored shower enclosure flung back her reflection haloed in sunshine. Her hair gleamed, her skin glowed. Except for the thickness at her waist, she was slender and fit, the very picture of pregnant health, and any notion that she might miscarry preposterous. Yet, even as she admonished herself for overreacting, another cramp, so exactly fitting the description of contractions, built to a crescendo.

Her wail of distress brought Edmund fully awake and shoving open the door. "Jenna, are you okay?"

"I'm hurting," she whimpered, hunching over the vanity as the wave of pain washed over her.

"Where? Did you slip and fall? Damn these marble floors, anyway! They're an accident waiting to happ—!"

And then he saw the way she was holding herself, and realization dawned. The blood drained out of his face. "Oh, honey!" he exclaimed in hushed tones, reaching for her. "Oh, jeez! When did this start?"

"I don't know," she moaned, fighting tears. "Edmund, I think I'm losing my baby…."

"No, you're not!" he said fiercely, swinging her up into his arms and striding back to the bedroom. "I won't allow it, do you hear? You're going to be fine and so is the baby. I won't have it any other way!"

He found her silk robe and helped her put it on, stuffed her feet into a pair of sandals, and carried her out to the garage. "I'll phone the hospital and let them know to expect us,'' he told her, carefully settling her in the front seat of the Navigator. "Don't worry about a thing, sweet pea. I've got everything under control."

All except the pain, and that was something only she could manage. And she was doing so very poorly; was helpless to stem the tears streaming down her face. "I'm so sorry, Edmund," she sobbed, doubling over as another cramp took hold.

He didn't answer. Instead, he turned on the four-way flashers and sped toward the Peace Arch Hospital, fire in his eye as he punched in numbers on the car phone, and fury in his voice as he muttered, "Where the devil are the police when you need them?"

She was whisked into an examining room as soon as they arrived. "You stay put," the desk clerk ordered, when Edmund tried to follow. "I need some information from you before you go racing off. Your wife's in excellent hands and you'll only be in the way in there, so just cool your jets and have a seat."

From her cubicle down the hall, Jenna could hear him objecting. She suspected just about everyone in the hospital could. Under any other circumstances, she'd have found it amusing.

But there was nothing remotely funny about the dull ache which never quite went away.

"Are you going to be able to save my baby?" she asked the doctor in charge, when he'd concluded his preliminary examination.

"I'd better, if I value my right to practice medicine," he said wryly. "That husband of yours is loaded for bear!"

He made a few notes and issued instructions to a waiting nurse, then said, "I'm sending you for an ultrasound. In the meantime, I'm giving you something which should stop the cramping. It'll mean hooking you up to an IV, so you'll be here at least several hours and possibly longer. But the fetal heartbeat is strong and I'm pretty confident you won't miscarry. However, consider today's incident a warning, Mrs. Delaney, and start taking better care of yourself.''

"Do you think it could happen again?''

"Hopefully not. But I want you on bed rest for the next few days, just to be on safe side. You're only fourteen weeks along and a baby's survival chances are zero this early in the game.''

"What about working? I run a day-care center for preschoolers and it involves a certain amount of lifting.''

The privacy curtain swished aside to reveal a wild-eyed Edmund. "Not any longer it doesn't!" he declared, coming to the foot of the bed. "As of now, you're off the job.''

"I have to agree," the doctor said. "I don't know what you've been up to lately, Jenna, but it's my guess this whole scare could have been avoided if you hadn't taken on more than you could comfortably handle.'' He directed a telling glance at Edmund. "Maybe you both need to be made more aware of that fact. Stress isn't good for any of us. It's particularly bad for expectant mothers.''

A technician came by just then, and set up the IV. Shortly after, another who introduced herself as Lisa took Jenna for the sonogram. Edmund stayed by her side the entire time, his hand clasping hers and his eyes tracking the images on the monitor as the examination proceeded.

Pointing to the tiny pulsing spot on the screen, Lisa said, "There's the heart…and that's the spine.''

Tense with anxiety, Jenna said "Do you see anything…?''

Lisa covered her with the sheet and prepared to leave.

"Everything looks fine to me, but the doctor will take a look and give you the final word.''

"This is all my fault,'' Edmund said, while they waited. "I've been pressuring you for days, and this last week's been a killer. Why didn't you make me back off?''

I tried to, and you wouldn't listen, she could have told him. But he looked so abjectly miserable that she hadn't the heart to come out and say so.

"If you'd lost the baby…" He closed his eyes and shook his head.

"You'd have married me for nothing," she teased, trying to lighten his mood.

If anything, her remark had the opposite effect. "Don't even think that! You're more to me than a baby machine, for God's sake!"

"How much more?" Appalled, she realized that, this time, she had voiced her thoughts aloud. Good grief, what had come over her? They *never* talked about their feelings— at least, not as they pertained to each other. Theirs was a marriage of utter convenience fortuitously made sweeter by sublime sex. Period!

Edmund looked equally shocked. "Well…enough," he blustered. "Enough that I…don't like seeing you with needles stuck in your arm and strangers poking around all over your body! What kind of question is that, anyway?"

The kind a woman asks when she realizes she's falling in love with a man who, when they're in bed, tells her she's beautiful and that he wants her, and that he misses her when they're not together, but who never allows himself to forget that the only reason they're married is for the sake of his children!

"I really don't know," she said, struggling to keep her feelings hidden. "It must be the medication they've given me. I'm not acting like myself at all."

Fortunately, the doctor came into the room just then and the awkward moment passed. "You're lucky, young woman. Your baby's a fighter and isn't going anywhere before the due date. But I'm keeping you here overnight anyway. You can go home tomorrow if there's no further sign of trouble *and* if you promise to behave yourself."

"Oh, she will," Edmund assured him. "I'll see to it. She won't lift a finger if I can help it."

"No need to go overboard, Mr. Delaney," the doctor said dryly. "Your wife's an intelligent woman. I'm sure she'll figure out her limits and stay within them."

Edmund looked mystified. "I don't think he likes me," he said, when they were alone again. "I wonder why?"

"Perhaps because you're so bossy," she suggested.

But he laughed, and she knew he didn't for a moment believe she meant it—or that it could possibly be true.

They led a pretty quiet life for the next month, even to the point that Edmund missed two weekend visits with Molly in order to stay close to Jenna. It was a serene and happy time, filled with a new closeness and a new depth of passion between them.

"I don't know what I'd do if anything happened to you," Edmund told her more than once, as they lay with their bodies still sweetly linked in the afterglow of loving. "My life has taken such a different turn because of you."

They finished furnishing their house, dined out often at one or other of the many restaurants along the seafront. If he never came right out and said, *I love you,* he showed it in a dozen other ways. When they took walks along the beach, he held her hand, or put his arm around what was left of her waist. He brought her flowers, exotic orchids and gorgeous bouquets of fragrant lilies and roses. He worried about her not overdoing things, and phoned her frequently during the day when he was at work, to make sure she was looking after herself properly.

During those weeks, Jenna convinced herself that the ties binding her to her husband no longer relied solely on the practicalities. True romance had come sneaking into the mix and turned their arrangement into a real marriage.

"It's time we let the families in on the pregnancy,"

Edmund announced one morning. "Hell, it's time we let the whole world know you're having my baby!"

His parents accepted the news with the same unquestioning warmth with which they'd received news of the marriage. "We're delighted for both of you," they said. "We'd love to buy something for the nursery, so please let us know what you'd like."

Adrienne, too, offered her congratulations. "She'll be thrilled," she told Edmund, when he asked how he thought Molly would take the news. "She's itching to be a big sister and has been asking for a baby brother or sister for ages."

"So that's what all the rush and secrecy was about," Jenna's mother said, when she heard. "No wonder you weren't interested in reconciling with poor Mark. I sometimes wonder if you ever think of anyone but yourself, Jenna. But I suppose, if you're happy, that's really all that matters, and it would seem that Edmund can afford to keep my grandchild in style. And speaking of money, Amber is desperately looking for a way to fund her stay in New York. Do you suppose Edmund…?"

Irene hired two permanent assistants to help out at the day-care center. "It'll never happen," she declared, when Jenna mentioned returning to work after the baby was born. "The way Edmund's hovering over you, anyone would think you're made of glass. He won't stand for you putting in the kind of hours this job requires."

Jenna suspected she was right. "Call and let me know if you decide to go out, and when you expect to be home," he insisted each weekday morning before he left the house. "Don't leave me wondering if you've passed out on the bathroom floor or something, and can't get to the phone to call for help."

When she suggested he was perhaps taking the role of protective husband to extremes, he said, "What's wrong with a man looking out for his wife and baby? I'd have thought, after the way Armstrong behaved, you'd appreciate knowing you've got a man who cares.''

That he *cared* was obvious. Sometimes, in the wild and pulsing excitement of making love, his emotions would spill over to the point that she even thought he might forget himself enough to tell her he loved her. But although he whispered that she was beautiful and desirable and that he couldn't get enough of her, he always stopped short of making that ultimate declaration.

It wasn't that he wouldn't say the word ''love.'' Far from it, in fact. He told her he loved seeing her pregnant, and watching the way she smiled to herself as she made things for the nursery; that he loved feeling the baby move inside her, and planning their future together. He just never said simply, ''I love you!''

It probably wouldn't have mattered to her quite so much if she hadn't found herself loving him beyond anything she'd ever known before.

''How'd you feel about having Molly come and spend a week with us?'' he asked her, after she received a clean bill of health at her next prenatal checkup. She was twenty weeks along by then, exactly at the midpoint of her pregnancy, and blooming with health. ''It'll be a change for her, and give Adrienne a bit of a break.''

Jenna welcomed the chance to bond with the little girl, but, ''Do you think she's ready to be away from familiar surroundings for that long?'' she said. ''Most children her age can manage only a day or two at a time before they get homesick.''

He shrugged. ''Only one way to find out. And it's not as if she'll be staying with strangers. We're her family, for Pete's sake.''

''We're already asking her to accept a lot of changes, Edmund, what with me being your wife and a baby on the way. I'm not sure it's fair to push too hard until she's had time to adjust.''

"And I'm not sure I want to risk your well-being by having you traipsing around the Interior in the middle of the hottest September on record,'' he said irritably. "It won't hurt Adrienne to do the driving for once. I want to talk to her anyway, and it's impossible to get her alone at the farm without good old Bud horning in on the conversation.''

Jenna sometimes thought that Edmund's antipathy for Bud had less to do with the part he'd played in Molly's accident than it had with the fact that he was married to Adrienne. "He strikes me as a very decent man,'' she said. "And he clearly adores Molly.''

"Nevertheless he's not her father, and what I have to say to Adrienne is no concern of his.''

"Is it any of mine?'' she asked, taken aback by his caustic dismissal of the man who certainly filled the role of surrogate parent in Molly's life, even if he wasn't related to her by blood.

"You've got plenty of other things on your mind. How's the knitting going? Are you going to have that blanket finished before the baby gets here?''

He was the most candid man she'd ever known, yet in the last week or two he'd several times been unavailable when she'd done as he asked and phoned him during the day. "I had an appointment and turned off my phone,'' he'd say, when she questioned him about it; or, "You'd hung up before I could answer, but I got back to you fairly quickly, and that's all that matters.''

They were, like everything else he did, eminently reasonable responses, yet she'd been left with the uneasy feeling that he wasn't being entirely open with her. For him now to deflect her question by trying to change the subject troubled her more than a little.

"Making things for the baby doesn't render me mentally

defective, Edmund. I'm still capable of sharing your concerns.''

He dropped a kiss on her head. ''You're supposed to avoid stress, sweet pea.''

''If you believe that, then stop keeping me in the dark. You're being evasive, and it's not like you. There's more behind this sudden interest in having Molly stay with us, and I want to know what it is.''

He threw up his hands. ''Okay! If you must know, I'm not convinced she's getting the best follow-up care from the accident. She's supposed to be getting therapy three times a week, but whenever I ask how it's going, I don't get a straight answer. There've been too many postponements, last-minute switches in scheduling, for my peace of mind. So I'm doing my own follow-up, and taking her to see a pediatric orthopedist here in the city. I want a second opinion on her progress from someone with no ax to grind.''

''You're being unfair to Adrienne,'' Jenna protested. ''The only time she canceled a therapy appointment that I'm aware of was when Molly came down with that cold.''

''What about the time she missed a whole week of aqua-therapy?''

''That wasn't Adrienne's fault! The public pool was closed because of some maintenance problem. What was she supposed to do about it—get Bud to bulldoze a hole in the back garden and fill it with water?''

She was treading on delicate ground, of course, and Edmund wasted no time calling her on it. ''You know something, Jenna? It really ticks me off that you think you know more about my ex-wife than I do, when the most time you've ever spent with her is twenty minutes.''

''That's not true. We've spoken on the phone several times.''

''Fine,'' he said. ''Make it an hour! It still doesn't compare to the five years I lived with her. Ever since she remarried, she wanders around like a latter-day sixties' flower child, off in la-la land half the time, full of peace and love, and live and let live. I sometimes wonder what else they're growing up there beside grapes!''

''Whether or not you approve of her or her choice of mate, Adrienne loves Molly and she'd never neglect her.''

''That's easy for you to say. It's not your daughter we're talking about.''

Jenna took a deep breath and folded her hands over her stomach. ''It would seem you've built up quite a head of resentment in the last little while, and since you seem bent on airing your grievances, I've got one I'd like to throw into the mix. I'm fully aware that Molly is nobody's child but yours. I'd have a hard time forgetting, given the number of times you remind me. What I'd like to know, though, is if you don't want me to treat her as if she were mine as well, why did you bother to marry me in the first place?''

He made a visible effort to rein in his annoyance. ''I'm surprised you have to ask me that, considering you won't be able to get through a door sideways before much longer because you're pregnant with my child,'' he said, patting her belly possessively. ''And I don't mean to shut you out. I'm just following doctor's orders and doing my best to keep your life stress free. If you don't feel up to having Molly here—''

''I never even hinted at that!'' she said, refusing to be thrown off-track by such an absurd suggestion. ''I merely expressed some concern that she might get homesick. But I'll bow to your superior wisdom and settle for doing my level best to make sure she has a lovely time while she's with us.''

''Thank you, sweet pea. You're the best.''

''In fact,'' she said, annoyed enough by his complacent smile to want to get in a sly dig of her own, ''I'll prepare a room for Adrienne, as well. She won't want to drive both

ways in one day, and having her here overnight might make
the transition a bit easier for Molly.''

''Oh, terrific! My current wife and my ex both under the
same roof! As if I don't have enough to deal with, without
that!''

But it was Bud who ended up driving Molly down to the
coast. A big, bearded man wearing denim shorts, sandals,
and a baseball cap, he arrived in a pickup truck with Molly
tucked into the small back seat of the cab. ''Adrienne's a
bit under the weather,'' he explained, shifting nervously
from one foot to the other. ''She gone and hurt her back
gardening, so your timing couldn't have worked out better.
Not having Molly around will give her a chance to rest up
a bit.''

''I'm glad we're able to help,'' Jenna said and ignoring
Edmund's black look, went on, ''It's a long trip back, so if
you'd like to stay here tonight and get an early start tomorrow, you're welcome to do so. We've got plenty of room.''

''Thanks anyway, but I'll push off. Don't like leaving
Adrienne alone when she can't get about very good. We're
pretty isolated if anything went wrong and she needed
help.''

''Well,'' Jenna said, bending a meaningful glance
Edmund's way, ''I'm sure my husband agrees with you. He
acts like a trained guard dog around me sometimes! But can
we at least offer you something to eat or drink before you
start back?''

''Aw, I'll stop somewhere along the way. But thanks.''
He bent down and hugged Molly. ''You be good, Moll, and
I'll see you next week. Don't forget you can phone us any
time you get lonely. And you take care of yourself, you
hear?''

She nodded, planted a kiss on Bud's cheek, then wriggled
free and scooted inside to explore the house.

''Pity he didn't show the same concern when he backed

a tractor over her,'' Edmund observed darkly, watching him drive away.

"I don't understand why you're so hard on him," Jenna said. "You ought to be happy that he cares so much for his wife."

"Give me a break, Jenna! The guy's an idiot. You've only got to listen to him and look at him to see that."

"I might be inclined to think you're jealous if it weren't that I'm sure you're above such petty emotion," she couldn't help saying. "Would you view him more kindly if he weren't married to your ex-wife?"

"I don't give a flying fig who Adrienne's married to! It's my daughter I'm concerned about."

"Well, I say you're worrying needlessly. Bud's tastes might not be as sophisticated as yours, and he might mangle the language a bit, but he strikes me as a very kind and caring man."

"Sweet pea," Edmund said, wrapping an arm around her shoulder and giving her a squeeze, "you'd find something good to say about the devil himself. Just as well you've got me around to set you straight! Let's go get Molly settled, then I'll firm up her appointment with the specialist."

Dr. James Franklin was old enough to satisfy parents that he knew his business, and youthful enough to inspire trust in his young patients. "I'd like to have a look at some X rays to be on the safe side," he told Edmund and Jenna, when he'd finished examining Molly, "but from everything I've seen, I'd say your daughter's treatment coincides exactly with what I'd have prescribed."

"But she's favoring one leg over the other," Edmund said. "At this rate, she'll walk with a limp for the rest of her life."

"As her recovery progresses, and provided you're diligent with the physiotherapy, that will correct itself. In the meantime, what you have to take into account is the residual emotional trauma she's undergone and not pile on the pressure too much. Let her advance at her own speed and be sure to give her the kind of reassurance she needs.''

''What about the muscle atrophy?''

''It's normal after a long period in a cast. The condition will reverse itself. Has already begun to do so, in fact. There's no evidence of nerve damage—not that I'd expect to find any at her age. That's the thing with children, Mr. Delaney. They show amazing recuperative powers.''

''What about long-term complications?''

''Long-term?'' Jenna thought the doctor looked taken aback by the question, which wasn't surprising. She thought he'd made it very clear there wouldn't *be* any long-term complications. But from the moment they'd stepped into the consulting room, Edmund had seemed bent on finding some. ''None. We're dealing with very young bones which heal well.''

''So you're willing to guarantee she'll grow up to lead a perfectly normal life?''

Again, the doctor looked puzzled. *''Normal?''*

''Be able to have children,'' Edmund said impatiently. ''There was pelvic injury as well as that to her legs.''

''I'm a doctor, not a fortune teller, Mr. Delaney, and contrary to popular belief, medicine is not an exact science. So, no, I can't guarantee she'll one day bear you beautiful grandchildren, any more than I guarantee she'll marry a man you approve of. What I can do is state categorically that your daughter is making a good recovery from her accident.''

''But not that she'll be as good as new?''

The doctor scratched his head. ''I'd rather she hadn't been injured in the first place, if that's what you're asking me. Certainly she hasn't benefitted from the experience. No child—or adult for that matter—is better off as a result of her kind of physical and emotional trauma, and I certainly don't recommend you expose her to the same kind of risk in the future. The outcome this time could have been vastly more tragic and she might not be so lucky again.''

For the first time since the examination had begun, Edmund appeared satisfied. "I believe you've given me the answers I was looking for, Dr. Franklin," he said, rising from his chair and reaching across the desk to shake the specialist's hand. "Thank you very much for seeing us.''

They drove to Stanley Park afterward, and had a picnic lunch at the playground near Second Beach. Edmund was in fine spirits, making Molly laugh by hand-feeding the ducks and then pretending to be scared of the Canada geese, and making no mention of the interview. But the minute she hobbled off to ride the swings, he said to Jenna, "Well, you heard the man.''

"What I heard," Jenna said flatly, "was you looking for reasons to level criticism at the way Adrienne and Bud are looking after Molly.''

"I'm building a case, sweet pea," he replied, seeming not at all upset that she wasn't exactly cheering him on. "We're talking about my daughter's future here and I intend to use every bit of ammunition I can lay hands on.''

"Does her mother know you planned to take her to see another doctor?''

"No. Technically, we have joint custody. I don't need Adrienne's permission, nor can I imagine she'd refuse it even if I did.''

"If Molly were my child," Jenna said, ever mindful of her delicate role in the little girl's life, "I'd resent finding out after the fact, and I'd definitely suspect you were hiding something.''

There was a distinct chill in his voice when he spoke next. "I see. So what would you like me to do, Jenna? Come right out and admit I'm building a case to gain primary custody of Molly, and keep Adrienne informed each step of the way? Possibly hire a lawyer to prepare a counterattack on her behalf?"

"She's a mother, Edmund, and anyone can see that she loves Molly. I think she'll be devastated when she finds out what you're up to."

"But I'm just the father and how I feel doesn't count, is that it?"

"No!" she cried, wishing he weren't always so primed to take offence on the subject. "I don't mean that at all. But I wonder if your motivation is quite as selfless as you make it out to be."

"Exactly what are you implying?"

"Edmund, Dr. Franklin said nothing to indicate that Molly wasn't given the best possible care. Quite the opposite, in fact. Yet you persisted in badgering him—trying to get him to say something, *anything,* which you could use to label Adrienne and Bud as unfit parents."

"And your point is?" he said coldly.

"There must have been a report filed at the time of the accident and since you're not waving it in the air like some sort of trophy, I assume it contained nothing to indicate they were guilty of criminal negligence." She sighed. "Accidents happen, Edmund, even with the most vigilant supervision. With children, they happen in a split second. You know that."

"What I know," he said, his voice dangerously intent, "is that my daughter could have died and I'll move heaven and earth before I leave her open to the same risk again."

"And if you don't succeed?"

He fixed her in a killing glare, one so ruthless that she flinched. "But I've already taken steps to ensure that I do," he said. "I married you, sweet pea."

"I realize I'm just the means to an end," she said, stifling the hurt his cold assessment provoked, "but I'd hoped there might be more to our...*arrangement* than pure convenience. I'd hoped that by now we'd have developed..."

"What?"

"A mutual respect. A shared..." Once again she hesitated, afraid to voice what had been in her heart for weeks.

"A shared what?" His tone expressed nothing but amused cynicism. "Love? Is that the word you're looking for?"

"Would it be so terrible if I were?"

"It would be disastrous. A moment ago you quite rightly referred to our marriage as an *arrangement.* Start clouding the issue with ideas of love and our whole plan of action is jeopardized. People don't think straight once they let their emotions take over."

"That doesn't seem to concern you much when we're in bed. It doesn't impair your performance at all. In fact, there've been times when I've wondered if we aren't falling a little bit in love with each other."

"Jenna, Jenna, Jenna!" He shook his head in mock despair. "We can *make love* till our eyeballs rattle, but that doesn't translate into our *being* in love. At your age, surely you know that one has nothing to do with the other?"

"Well, if I didn't before, I do now," she said, a great well of misery bursting inside.

As if realizing he'd cut her to the quick, he patted her hand. "Don't go all soft and sentimental on me at this late date, sweet pea. Look how well we've managed so far by not allowing our hearts to rule our heads. We need to hang together now, more than ever."

There were a dozen replies she could have made; things like, *You need me a lot more than I need you, Edmund Delaney, so don't go giving me orders on how I'm supposed to feel and what I'm supposed to do. If I walk out on you, you'll be up the creek without the proverbial paddle!* Instead, she said starchily, "I'd appreciate it very much if you wouldn't call me 'sweet pea.'"

"Sure." He shrugged. "Whatever you say. Anything, as long as you don't lose sight of the true objective here, which is that *both* my children know who their father is, and that everything he does is in their best interests." He got up from the picnic bench and brushed a few crumbs off the leg of his pants. "If we don't want to get caught in rush hour traffic, we should start heading home. Want a hand packing up here?"

"No," she said. At that moment, she didn't want a thing from him because it struck her suddenly that although he could be generous to a fault, in the end, he exacted a price for everything he gave, whether it was material comfort or emotional support.

One of the reasons he'd mentioned having Molly stay in town with them had been to give Adrienne a break from looking after her. As soon as he'd achieved that objective, though, the whole tenor of the visit had changed and taken on subversive undertones that made Jenna part of a conspiracy which left a very bad taste in her mouth.

He seemed able to read the doubts churning in her mind. "Don't look at me as if I've just sprouted horns," he said teasingly. "I don't have any diabolical plans up my sleeve. Nothing's changed since the day I proposed we get married."

"Yes, it has," she said coldly. "You led me to believe that Molly needed rescuing from an untenable situation with your ex-wife when, in fact, no such situation exists and what you really want to do is punish Adrienne for daring to make a life without you."

His gaze went flat and inscrutable. "I don't have to prove myself to you, Jenna, not where Molly's concerned. But I will remind you that *you* are now my wife, so regardless of what you think you know, you owe loyalty to *me*, not Adrienne."

"Your wife?" she echoed bitterly. "Oh, please! I'm no

more than a necessary accessory. Once I've served my purpose, you'll probably discard me like an old shoe.''

''Dream on, my dear. I don't part willingly with what I consider to be mine. And you can bet your last dollar that, regardless of the outcome of Molly's living arrangements, I'm not about to be shunted out of my second child's life. Whether or not you like it, we're married. For better or for worse.''

For all that the day was brilliant with September sunshine, a cold chill ran over her at his words. Once she'd found comfort in knowing she was married to a man with the courage of his convictions. Now, it struck a disturbingly ominous note.

CHAPTER TEN

EVERY evening before she went to bed, Molly phoned home to say good-night to her mother. Usually, Edmund took her into the den to make the call while Jenna cleaned up the kitchen.

The day they'd taken her to see the specialist though, Molly came skipping down the hall with her funny little lopsided gait, looking for Jenna who was loading dinner plates into the dishwasher. "I've finished on the phone but Mommy wants to talk to you now, Jenna."

"What's all this about Molly seeing a doctor?" Adrienne asked, coming straight to the point when Jenna picked up the extension in the kitchen. "Has something happened? Is she ill?"

Hearing the anxiety in the other woman's voice, Jenna hastened to reassure her. "She's perfectly fine, Adrienne."

"But you did take her to some doctor?"

"Well...yes."

"Why?"

"I think," Jenna said, more uncomfortable by the second at being the one having to field such pertinent questions, "you should be asking Edmund that."

"I'm asking you, Jenna," Adrienne said tensely. "What's going on out there? What's Edmund up to?"

"Nothing. He just...wanted to make sure he was doing everything possible to speed up Molly's recovery."

"Then why not ask me, since I'm the one who's in constant touch with her regular doctor? It doesn't add up that he'd call in someone else, unless she's had some sort of relapse."

155

"I promise you that's not the case," Jenna insisted. "Really, Adrienne, Molly's just fine."

"Why don't I quite believe this is all as innocent as you're making it out to be?"

Quite possibly because lying through my teeth makes me owly, Jenna thought frantically.

"Jenna? Are you still there?"

"Yes," she said miserably. "Adrienne, I wish you'd talk to Edmund about this. It really isn't up to me to be explaining…things."

"So there *is* something to explain! I thought as much. Well, put him on the line then, because I'm not hanging up until I've got to the bottom of whatever scheme he's hatching."

"He's trying to be a good father, that's all."

"Hah! Edmund's idea of being a good father is to treat his daughter as if she were part of his expensive inventory. She's just another commodity to him."

"You're not being fair, Adrienne!"

"No? You'll change your tune once your own child is born. I'm warning you, Jenna, he'll try to take over every aspect of that baby's life unless you put your foot down at the start. It's the chief reason our marriage broke up, though I don't suppose he's told *you* that. Edmund collects people the way others collect china, a piece at a time. And heaven help anyone who comes between him and his next acquisition. He's a control freak, pure and simple."

Shockingly, Edmund's voice responded to that, filtering down the line from the phone still off the hook in the den. "Thanks for the endorsement, Adrienne. I'm sure my wife feels a whole lot better now that she's heard your version of what being married to me is all about. Just what the hell do you think you're trying to do—sabotage this relationship, too?"

"Never mind taking umbrage at me," she snapped back.

"You're the one with some explaining to do. What's behind this mysterious visit to a doctor and why wasn't I informed about it beforehand?"

"For the same reason that you waited nearly twelve hours before you let me know that Molly had been almost crushed to death under the wheels of a tractor—there was nothing you could have done about it. I decided I wanted a second opinion on her condition and I was well within my rights to seek one without asking your permission first."

"The only reason it took me so long to get in touch with you when she was hurt," Adrienne said bitterly, "is that, despite all your carrying on about what a dedicated father you are and how you always have Molly's welfare in mind, you left town without letting me know where you were, and I had to wait until somebody answered the phone in the warehouse the next morning, to find out how to get in touch with you."

Too sick at heart to listen to any more, Jenna quietly hung up the kitchen phone. Adrienne had struck a disconcerting chord with her assessment of Edmund, reinforcing suspicions which, for all that she tried to deny them, had been flourishing at the back of Jenna's mind for some time and which, after that afternoon's confrontation, had burst into full bloom.

Sadly, Edmund's regard for Molly *did* spring from something more than fatherly concern. It had to do with winning, with proving himself an unbeatable opponent. It had to do with punishing Adrienne because *she* was the primary parent and *he* had been relegated to a less prominent role. What was best for Molly, or where she would be happiest, had become lost in a game of one-upmanship in which that poor little girl was nothing but a pawn, a trophy to be won.

A tug at her skirt made Jenna look down to find Molly leaning against the counter. "Why is Daddy mad?" she inquired anxiously. "Why is he saying bad things to Mommy?"

"Grown-ups sometimes say things they don't mean, darling," she said, kneeling down and scooping the child into her arms. "Daddy has been worried about you, that's all."

"Is he going to make me leave Mommy and stay here?"

Dear God in heaven, what was she supposed to do? Tell the truth and say that might very well be the case? She couldn't, not if her life depended on it! "No, darling. You'll be going home to Mommy in a few days."

Molly popped her thumb into her mouth and regarded her seriously. Then, she leaned her head against Jenna's shoulder and gave a heartfelt little sigh. "I want to go home now," she quavered. "I miss Mommy and Poppa Bud."

Jenna's heart ached for her. "It's too late to drive such a long way tonight, Molly. How about if I read you a story after your bath, instead, then tomorrow, if you still want to go home, we'll talk to Daddy about it?"

"There won't be any need because it's not going to happen," Edmund said from the doorway. "And I'll thank you, Jenna, not to go making promises you can't keep."

Struggling to her feet with Molly hanging on like a barnacle clinging to a rock, Jenna said warningly, "Now isn't the time or place to discuss it, Edmund. This child's had enough for one day."

"Then hand her to me and I'll put her to bed."

Though every instinct screamed for her to thwart him, to hold Molly close and rock her to sleep in her arms if that's what it would take to soothe the little thing, Jenna did as she was told. Poor Molly was already being pulled in two different directions, without her adding a third.

Too discouraged to care that there were still things needing to be cleaned up in the kitchen, she went out to the patio and lowered herself into a chair. Her back ached and her ankles were puffy, but they were minor discomforts and quickly remedied with a warm bath and a good night's sleep.

But the real hurting—that great load of pain that started somewhere in the region of her heart and spread until it consumed every inch of her—*that,* she could do nothing to ease. Propping her elbow on the table, she leaned her head wearily in her hand and wondered yet again what spark of madness had ever led her to believe two people could base a marriage on total unfamiliarity, and expect to make it work. She didn't feel like a wife; she felt like a mouse desperately racing down blind alleys as it tried to find its way out of a maze.

"Is she asleep?" she asked, when Edmund finally reappeared.

"She is. No thanks to you, though." He flung himself down opposite her. "And what's with this business of her sucking her thumb? She stopped that over a year ago."

"It's her way of showing us she's upset. Children her age are apt to revert to earlier habits when their security's threatened. She heard you and Adrienne arguing."

"Because you made it your business to tell her mother we'd been to see a specialist," he said bitterly. "What were you thinking of, tipping my hand like that?"

"Adrienne heard the news from Molly. It wouldn't have come as such a shock though, if you'd done the decent thing and discussed it with her first."

"And what else did you see fit to let drop? That you thought I was being sneaky and let's see…how did you put it earlier this afternoon?" He tapped one finger against his front teeth and pretended to look thoughtful. "Ah, yes. Now I remember—'that my motivation wasn't quite as selfless as I made it out to be'?"

"I didn't have to," she said. "Adrienne's already figured out that much for herself. She thinks you're overly possessive about Molly, and she's right. But you don't care about that child nearly as much as you think you do. You've got an imagined score to settle with Adrienne and her husband, and you're using Molly to do it.''

''What a charming thing to say—and this from the woman who only hours ago was chirping on about falling in love!''

''I see now that I was merely deluding myself. All these weeks—'' her voice broke, and she gulped, furious to find herself on the brink of tears ''—I thought we were forging something worth hanging on to. I thought we were growing closer, that we were learning to trust each other. But how can I trust a man I no longer believe in?''

''No longer believe in?'' he exploded. ''What the devil do you mean by that?''

Tears pooled along her lower eyelids, blurring his image and turning him into a mirage in much the same way that the inner man was showing himself to be. ''You aren't who I thought you were,'' she whispered, a deep and painful sorrow ripping her apart. ''I don't know you. I never did.''

''Don't give me that! I was up-front with you from the very first. You got exactly what you were looking for when you married me, and so, I thought, did I.''

''Then it appears we were both mistaken.''

''Why? Because we happen to disagree over one little thing?'' He slapped the flat of his hands on the tabletop, so hard the sound ricocheted over the patio like a rifle shot. ''For God's sake, Jenna, where's your sense of proportion?''

''Right where it should be,'' she cried, the tears falling fast and furious. ''Because this isn't 'one little thing.' A child's future is at stake, and I won't help you perpetuate the myth that you're doing her a favor by taking her away from her mother. I will not be part of any scheme that removes that little girl from the only home she knows or cares about.''

''You will do,'' he said, with chilling emphasis, ''exactly what you agreed to do when you married me. You saved face by producing a respectable husband just when you needed one, and in return I got a wife ably qualified to help me win court approval to bring my daughter to live with me, instead of with some hayseed farmer who damn near killed her.''

''When are you going to stop laying blame and accept that what happened was an accident? What's it going to—?''

''I don't give a rat's ass what you want to call it, my dear. Accident, negligence, stupidity—they all add up to the same thing in the end. My daughter almost lost her life, and I'll see you in hell before I let you stand in the way of my preventing that from ever happening again.''

''How do you propose to do that, Edmund?'' she said, her chin quivering uncontrollably. ''By gagging me before I take the witness stand? Because that's about the only way you're going to keep me from speaking my mind.''

''You owe me your allegiance.''

''*Allegiance?*'' She choked back a bitter laugh. ''Is that what this marriage is all about—me bending the knee to you? What happened to respect for the other person's point of view? What happened to honesty?''

He lunged out of the chair and loomed over her. ''You're a fine one to ask! What happened to the promises you made to me on our wedding day?''

''To love and honor, you mean? We opted for a very brief ceremony so they never arose and for that, at least, I'm deeply grateful. It spares me having to break my word. As for the 'obey' part, it went by the wayside years ago when more enlightened men than you've turned out to be recognized that women and children weren't chattels.''

''What about the other promises, those we exchanged in private, when you purported to assist me every way you could in my efforts to win the custody suit?''

She hauled herself out of her chair also, and gave him

back glare for glare. "Those I made in ignorance of the true state of affairs. Consequently, I no longer feel bound by them."

"I'm holding you to them, anyway, Jenna. I won't allow you to walk away from them."

Won't allow...how often had she heard him use those words? Almost as often as he referred to Molly as *his* daughter, as if she were a possession to which only he had entitlement.

Edmund collects people the way others collect china, one piece at a time, Adrienne had said. *I'm warning you, Jenna...he's a control freak, pure and simple....*

And she was a fool not to have recognized sooner that in marrying him she had merely exchanged one set of problems for another, much more serious predicament.

Still, she made one last effort to put right what had gone so dreadfully wrong. "Edmund," she said, appealing to him with outstretched hands, "please, I'm begging you! Drop the idea of taking Molly away from Adrienne. She's a good mother. She doesn't deserve this. You and I have so much— a beautiful home which can be a haven of warmth and welcome for Molly any time she wants to come here, a baby on the way, a future which, if we work together, could be better than either of us ever envisaged when we first decided to get married. *Please,* let it be enough!"

For a moment, she thought she'd reached him. His eyes were tortured, his mouth clamped tight in misery. But in the end, he shook his head and turned away from her. "I can't," he said.

Jenna slept in one of the spare rooms that night. She didn't trust herself to lie beside him and not succumb to the raging need to find comfort in his arms. He didn't try to dissuade her. Without either of them coming out and saying so, they both knew they'd passed a point of no return and that making love wouldn't fix what was broken between them.

Some time around three in the morning, she was awoken by a thin cry coming from Molly's room. The poor little thing was probably dreaming, she thought, hurrying next door to comfort her.

But Molly was wide-awake and standing on the floor. "I went wee-wee in the bed," she wailed, shrinking away when Jenna tried to pick her up. "I'm all wet."

"Oh, darling, don't cry. It's okay! We'll get you cleaned up and dry in no time." Gently, she took the child's hand and led her to the bathroom across the hall. "Let me sponge you off, then we'll put on clean pajamas."

"But my bed's wet as well."

"Never mind about that old bed. I'll take care of it in the morning, and you can sleep with me for the rest of the night."

She'd hoped they wouldn't disturb Edmund but he must have been sleeping as poorly as she because he came staggering out of his room just as she was carrying Molly to hers. "What's going on? Is Molly sick?"

"No," she said. "Just a little nighttime accident, that's all."

"She wet the bed?" He sounded amazed; insulted even.

"It happens," Jenna told him. "It's no big deal."

"I guess not." But he wasn't convinced, as his next question proved. "Isn't she a bit old to be doing that, though?"

"No," she said again and gave him a level look. "Nor do I think we need to belabor the subject now. She's embarrassed enough as it is."

"So where are you taking her?" he said, when he saw that she wasn't going back to Molly's room.

"To sleep with me."

"There's no need for that. Give her to me. She can spend

the rest of the night in our bed. God knows, there's enough room in it tonight.''

But Molly, who'd been drooping sleepily on Jenna's shoulder, buried her face more tightly against her neck. "No," she mumbled. "I don't want to be with Daddy."

He deserved it, and more. Yet the desolation on his face spurred Jenna to dangerous pity. He *did* love his daughter, she knew. The trouble was, he couldn't bear to share her with others who also loved her.

"Give her to me, Jenna," he repeated, his voice raw with hurt.

"No," she said softly. "Not this time, Edmund. I won't let you upset her any more than she already is. Good night."

He was still standing where she'd left him when she turned into her own room. His hands hung helplessly at his sides, his hair was all rumpled from sleep, and he wore a look of stunned disbelief. Not only had his daughter rejected him, his wife had dared to defy him, too. And he obviously hadn't the foggiest idea why they'd resort to such extreme measures when, in his view, all he was trying to do was be a good father.

After a strained breakfast the next morning, Edmund put Molly through her paces in the pool while Jenna took a shower. The light on the answering machine was blinking when she came out of the bathroom, and a man identifying himself as Jason Phillips had left a message.

"I've managed to get us a court hearing for the end of the week, which doesn't leave us much time to fine-tune our strategy, Edmund," he said, "so we need to get together, this morning if possible, to go over the final details. I want your wife here, too, because she's crucial to the whole undertaking, and since you've got the child staying with you, I'd like to talk to her as well. Might as well line up as much ammunition as we can, so get back to me, and we'll set up an appointment.''

Although he didn't say so, it was clear enough that Mr. Phillips was a lawyer. And equally clear that, without ever mentioning it to her, Edmund had already set in motion the legal process by which he hoped to win custody of Molly, even to the point of manipulating events so that she was in town just when it would help him the most.

''What did you think I was going to do?'' he asked scornfully, when she challenged him on Mr. Phillips' role in the whole messy affair. ''Hire a plumber?''

''I'd hoped you'd be more open about what you were up to. Silly me, right?''

He rolled his eyes. ''Don't go making a big deal about nothing, for crying out loud! I was obeying doctor's orders, that's all, and saw no point in involving you when you already had enough on your mind with the baby.''

''How convenient!''

''If you were that anxious to know what was going on, all you had to do was ask. Not, I might add, that I feel under any obligation to give you an accounting of every minute of my working day.''

''I did ask,'' she reminded him. ''All those times I couldn't reach you, when you had your phone turned off—those special meetings you were so vague about—you were consulting with your lawyer, weren't you?''

''Yes. And I'll be consulting him again today. And so will you.''

''No,'' she said. ''I absolutely will not! You're on your own, Edmund, and you can glower until you turn blue in the face, but I'm not going to change my mind. *You* might not have any conscience, but I like to be able to look myself in the mirror and not cringe at what I see. And I will not be party to going behind Adrienne's back. Regardless of what you think of her as a mother, or of her choice of husband, she deserves better than to be ambushed like this.''

''What's gotten into you, Jenna?'' he roared, his face flushing with anger. ''To hear you talk, anyone would think you'd found yourself married to a kingpin of the underworld bent on unspeakable crime. I'm going after what's mine. Why is that so terrible?''

''Oh, Edmund!'' She buried her face in her hands, despair and frustration overwhelming her. ''What's terrible is that you even have to ask! You can't *own* people!''

''I don't mean it like that. Stop twisting my words.''

''Yes, you do mean it like that,'' she said hopelessly. ''You just don't understand—''

''No, I don't,'' he said, his voice tight with fury. ''So explain it to me. After everything I've heard you say about deadbeat dads who walk away from their kids and never look back, tell me why you refuse to support your own husband when all I'm doing is trying my best to take care of my daughter.''

''You're going about it the wrong way. She's not a corporate asset and this isn't—or shouldn't be—a hostile takeover. But I'm afraid that's what it's turned into, and I refuse to have any part of it.''

They had been lovers and she thought they'd been friends, but at that moment, as they stood facing each other, they were nothing but adversaries, unalterably opposed. One of them had to back down. But he would not, and she could not.

And so the silence spun out between them, each passing second filled with a rancor and resentment that sounded a death knell to any hope she'd had that their marriage would turn into something lasting or sublime.

At last, he said heavily, ''Fine. I'll do it without you.''

Bleakly, she watched as, his face set in lines of misery, he reached for the phone and arranged the requested appointment. Helpless to stop the process he'd begun, she stood by as he loaded Molly into the car. "Don't hold lunch for us," was all he said by way of goodbye. "I'm taking her shopping this afternoon and don't know when we'll be back."

The day dragged by. Too restless to settle, Jenna cleaned the house from one end to the other, all the while praying that Edmund would call to say he'd had a change of heart. When two o'clock came and went with still no word, she gave up waiting for miracles and went outside to do some gardening.

She was deadheading geraniums in the flower bed next to the front door when a vehicle turned into the driveway. It was not Edmund who rolled to a stop in front of the garage doors, but Bud behind the wheel of his pickup, with Adrienne seated next to him.

"We've come to take Molly home," she said, climbing down from the cab with obvious difficulty. "I don't know what Edmund's up to and I'm not waiting any longer to find out. I want my daughter. Now."

"I'm afraid," Jenna said, hating to find herself in the middle of the mess for all that she'd done her best to stay out of it, "she's out with her father."

"Out where?"

She couldn't meet the other woman's forthright gaze. "They went...shopping."

"Fine. We'll wait. And while we do, perhaps you'd be good enough to get her stuff together."

"I..."

"You have a problem doing that, Jenna?"

"No, of course not."

"Good. We'll be waiting in the truck."

Noticing the pinched look about Adrienne's mouth, and the way she squinted with pain as she massaged the small of her back, Jenna gestured toward the house. "At least come in and make yourselves comfortable while I pack her suitcase.''

She tried to sound casual, but Adrienne wasn't fooled for a minute. "We both know this isn't a social call, Jenna, so never mind being the perfect hostess. You don't want us in your home any more than I want my daughter in it.''

"Easy, hon. No point in taking it out on Jenna," Bud said, putting a restraining hand on her arm, then turned to Jenna apologetically. "She's not feeling too swift," he explained. "Back's still troubling her some.''

"I understand," Jenna said, feeling dreadfully sorry for the woman. "Adrienne, if you're not comfortable about coming into the house, at least have a seat in the back garden. You'll cook sitting in the truck in this weather.''

"I don't want to put you out.''

"You're not. I was about to take a break anyway, and make some iced tea. I wish you'd both join me.''

Adrienne bit her lip. "Well, since you're so determined to be gracious, do you happen to have any aspirin? My back really is killing me. Our old truck's no Cadillac, I'm afraid.''

Oh, my dear! Jenna thought, shepherding them both through the side gate and into the shade of the umbrella table on the patio, before going inside to make the tea, *it's going to take a lot more than a couple of aspirin to ease the pain you're about to have inflicted on you!*

When she came back out with glasses, a frosty pitcher of tea, and a bottle of aspirin, she found Adrienne lying back in a chaise, and Bud hovering attentively at her side. "This is real nice of you, Mrs. Delaney," he said. "The doc gave Adrienne some pills, but she's been in such a state ever since last night's phone call that she clean forgot to bring 'em with her when we set out this morning.''

"Yes," Adrienne put in. "I don't think either of us got a wink of sleep. But Bud's right—I shouldn't take it out on you. Molly told me you've been wonderful with her, and she's so excited about the new baby, she can hardly wait for him to be born. We've been working on a gift for him—nothing much, just pasta shells glued to an old picture frame, but she's thrilled to bits with it.''

Jenna's throat closed with shame and a haze of embarrassing tears filmed her eyes. To be faced with this woman's generosity of spirit toward her ex-husband's new family, and know that he was bent only on misplaced vengeance, grieved her beyond words.

Fortunately, she was spared having to reply by Edmund and Molly's return. The child gave a squeal of delight when she saw her mother and stepfather and letting go of her balloon, flung herself at them.

Excusing herself, Jenna muttered something about collecting the trowel she'd left in the front flower bed, but once through the side gate she kept going, up the drive and out to where a path cut down to the beach. Not only did she need time in which to compose herself, she had no wish to be part of the scene about to unfold. What Edmund was doing was wrong, but he was still her husband and she would not willingly condemn him in front of others.

The truck was gone when she came back an hour later, and so was Molly. Only Edmund remained, and he was primed for battle. ''I'm surprised you've got the guts to show your face around here after the stunt you just pulled,'' he greeted her.

''What have I done or said now to displease you?'' she asked wearily. ''Allowed Adrienne and Bud to set foot on *your* property? Let them sit in *your* chairs, drink from *your* glasses?''

''How about blatantly taking their side against mine, even to the point of having Molly's bag packed and ready to go, the minute I brought her home? Tell me, sweet pea, what other nasty little surprises are you waiting to spring on me when I'm least expecting them?''

CHAPTER ELEVEN

How well she'd perfected the art of injured innocence! Big gray eyes glistening, sweet mouth quivering slightly, she hovered in the doorway and looked at him as if he'd gone mad.

"I'm not the one hatching plots, Edmund," she said, her voice so full of sorrowful regret that he was glad she hadn't gone with him to speak to Jason Phillips. Even a lawyer as experienced as he would have been hard-pressed to see past the theatrics. As for how a judge might be taken in…!

"Can the performance, Jenna!" he rapped out. "This is me, remember? The man you married under false pretenses."

"If I did," she said, twisting her wedding ring agitatedly, "the falsehood was all yours. You misrepresented the true state of affairs with Adrienne."

"And you, being so much wiser than the rest of us poor mortals, took it upon yourself to rectify my mistake by betraying me, is that it?"

"No. I have not once betrayed you. As for mistakes, they have been all mine."

"Oh, gee," he sneered, resentment overwhelming him to the point that it practically seeped out of his pores, "you actually admit to being fallible? I'd never have guessed."

"I should have listened to my instincts, and not to you. Instead, I followed my heart."

He let out a bark of laughter. "What heart? The one which prompted you to race to the phone as soon as my back was turned, and tell Adrienne to get down here quick so that she could put a stop to what was taking place?"

"Is that what she told you?"

"She didn't mince words stating the obvious. She had too many other things to get off her chest. I'm sure you'll be happy to know that she plans to fight me every inch of the way."

"I can't believe that comes as any surprise to you, Edmund. What did you think she'd do? Hand over Molly without a word? She's a *mother,* for pity's sake, not a hired nanny who looked after your child until it was convenient for you to take over the job!" She cupped her hands over her swollen belly possessively. "I can understand that, even if you can't!"

"No doubt," he said bitterly, "you'll make an excellent witness for the defense."

She flinched, as if he'd hit her. And damn her, but he felt the pain as if it had been directed at him. "I was of the impression that a wife can't be forced to testify against her husband."

"Not even if she's convinced he's an unmitigated bastard?"

He heard her sudden intake of breath, saw the rush of tears in her eyes, and steeled himself to resist both. "I think you're a fine man in every other respect, Edmund. From the day we met, I've admired you. These months we've been married have been a gift I'd never expected, and one I'd hoped would prove durable enough to last a lifetime."

She was trying hard, but the tears got the better of her and her voice broke. "God help me, I've fallen in love with you."

"Then I shudder to think how you'd behave if you hated me!"

She crumpled against the door frame, and wiped the back of her hand over her face. "This isn't about you and me," she sobbed. "It's about a mother's right to her child, and a little girl's right to live where she's happiest."

If he'd been in his right mind, he'd have considered before he spoke again. But by the time that thought occurred, it was too late. "You make me very nervous, Jenna. The way you're talking, and the way you've acted lately leads me to think I should take steps to make sure I don't wind up losing *both* my children. Hell, I'm already paying astronomical legal fees, so I might as well get two for the price of one, wouldn't you say?"

The way the blood drained out of her face scared the living daylights out of him. "I didn't mean that," he said, reaching for her. "So help me, Jenna, that wasn't what I meant to say!"

She shrank away from him as if his touch were poison—and who could blame her? "But the thought was there. It had to be."

"No. You're my wife."

"So was Adrienne, once."

"You're nothing like her. I…" He spread his hands helplessly, refusing to say aloud the words that had sprung to mind. *I care about you more than I ever cared about her!* Refusing even to admit them to himself. Men did and said crazy things sometimes. Hell, he was living proof of that! And things were already complicated enough.

But she was wilting as if all the life had been sapped out of her; as if the will to go on, to persevere despite their differences, had run its course. Something vital and lovely was withering inside her—not the baby, but something intangible that he suddenly realized was too precious and rare to be allowed to slip away without a fight. He was losing her as surely as if she were dying and suddenly he was willing to go to any lengths to save her.

"I love you," he said, the words seeming to tear loose from every artery and ligament in his body. Love hadn't been part of the plan; he had not seen it coming and he didn't know how to deal with it.

"If you love me," she said, "then stop this insane vendetta against Adrienne. Be satisfied with what you've got."

Any length but that! "Don't," he begged. "Sweetheart, don't ask me to trade one thing for another."

"All right," she said dully. "I won't."

Slowly, she straightened to her full height and smoothed the thin fabric of her maternity dress over her belly. When she turned to leave, he caught a brief glimpse of her in profile and it was like seeing her for the first time—the long, elegant neck, the graceful sweep of her hair, the sweet curve of her breasts, her proud, erect posture.

He had always thought her beautiful but pregnancy had endowed her with a luminescence that lent another dimension to her loveliness. It clutched at his gut, at his heart, and the impact staggered him.

"Where are you going?" he asked her.

"To make dinner."

"Let me. It's been one hell of a day and you look worn-out."

She signified agreement with a tilt of her shoulder so slight it was barely there at all.

That night, he tried every way he knew how to show her that she could trust him. She lay in his arms and let him kiss her, caress her, touch her all over with his hands and his mouth and his tongue. When he entered her, she accepted him; even held him as the passion escalated to a fine torture before smashing him to pieces and rendering him weak as a child. Even stroked his hair as he lay, spent, beside her.

The next day when he came home from work, she was gone.

For more than two weeks, she traveled, driving inland, discovering places which previously had been nothing but names on the map, and never staying more than one night in the same spot: north through Lillooet, then over to the old gold rush trail to Hundred Mile House, with a side trip east to Barkerville, where early signs of winter left the mornings sharp with frost. From there, north and west again on the Yellowhead Highway through Vanderhoof and past the Seven Sisters Peaks until she reached Prince Rupert on the cold and rainy north coast.

Finally, toward the end of a stormy day in the middle of October, she ended up back where everything had started, at The Inn on the west coast of Vancouver Island. She checked in, unpacked her bags, and although she wasn't particularly hungry, went down for dinner because she knew she was doing neither herself nor her baby any favors by missing meals.

Candlelight illuminated the dining room, enhanced by the logs blazing in the hearth. Rain lashed at the night-dark windows. Crystal clinked against crystal, waiters poured wine and obliged guests by taking photographs. And she, again, was alone. More alone than she'd ever been in her life.

"Will there be just one for dinner, madam?" the maître d'inquired, politely ignoring the fact that she was noticeably pregnant.

It was pure bad luck that he showed her to the same table she'd occupied the first time she'd been there, thereby stirring up the most wrenching sense of déjà vu. And equally unfortunate that at Edmund's old table sat a honeymoon couple so besotted with each other's company that they couldn't take their eyes off each other.

She had thought putting some distance between her and Edmund would perhaps give her a different perspective, one that would allow them to find some middle ground from which to rebuild their marriage. But she'd covered hundreds of miles since the morning she'd left him with nothing but a note to explain her decision, and the only conclusion she'd reached was that there *was* no middle ground. They were unalterably opposed.

No use telling herself that he wasn't deliberately trying to be evil or destructive. She knew that, as far as Molly was concerned, he honestly believed that what he was doing was right. But even if Jenna could have ignored the dictates of her own conscience which told her he was wrong, she could never forget his threat to take her own baby away from her.

That he'd spoken the words in anger, and tried to atone for them by telling her he loved her—words she'd longed to hear!—and by making love to her with an unguarded passion he'd never shown before, did nothing to alter the fact that he'd planted a fear so deep and powerful that it haunted her dreams and plagued her every waking minute.

Pushing aside the salad she'd ordered, she faced up to what she'd known for days: the marriage was over and the decent thing was to tell him so. In the note she'd left for him, she'd asked that he not try to find her, that he give her time to sort out her feelings, and he'd honored her request. In all fairness, he now had the right to know she was not coming back to him.

She phoned him the minute she got back to her room. He answered on the second ring and the sound of his voice did terrible damage to her resolve; so terrible that she could not at first bring herself to speak to him.

"Jenna?" he said, when the silence had lasted too long. "Sweetheart, is that you?"

"Yes," she finally croaked past the aching lump in her throat.

"*Thank God!* Honey, how are you and when are you coming home?"

"I'm not," she managed through the tears choking her. "That's why I'm calling, Edmund—to tell you that I won't be coming back."

"Not ever?" She heard the incredulity in his tone, could almost see the disbelief on his face. "Honey, you don't mean that. We can work this out. I've—"

"No," she said. "I'm afraid we can't. And the reason I'm calling you now is to tell you I intend filing for divorce, because I don't want you to hear it first from a lawyer."

"You're quite sure that's what you want, are you?"

Sure? No! How could any woman be sure that ending a relationship to the man she loved despite everything was what she really wanted? "I'm resigned to the inevitable," she said. "We've reached an impasse and I see no way for us to get past it. I'm afraid divorce is the only option."

"Fine. Then you can tell me so to my face. We're talking about ending a marriage, Jenna, not canceling a magazine subscription. A phone call just won't cut it."

She *couldn't* see him again, not yet! Not until her heart had mended a little. "I'm afraid it will have to," she said, and quickly, before she fell victim to his further persuasion, she broke the connection, then contacted the front desk and asked not to have any calls put through to her room.

It was only a little after seven o'clock, too early to think about going to bed even if she could have slept. As often happened in the evening, the baby was particularly active. Usually, it made her smile but tonight it merely reminded her that this would be yet another child growing up without a father.

Hugging her elbows, she paced to the window. Floodlights at the base of the building showed the trees bending before the onslaught of wind and rain, and great curtains of spray crashing over the rocks below. She was still standing there, mesmerized by the violence of the scene, when one of the hotel employees showed up at her door.

"Sorry to disturb you, ma'am, but there's some concern that we might lose power if this storm keeps going, so I've brought you candles and extra wood. I'll be happy to start a fire, if you like, and suggest that if you're thinking of ordering anything from room service, you do so now."

"Perhaps I will," she said, as a particularly vicious blast of wind shook the walls. "Some tea, perhaps."

"I'll have it sent up right away, ma'am. And the fire?"

"Yes," she said. "A fire would be nice."

"And a lot more cheerful than sitting in the dark, should that happen. At least you'll be warm."

In body, maybe. But neither a roaring fire nor a pot of hot tea could chase away the chill in her heart—nothing except the feel of Edmund's arms around her and that, sadly, was too risky a venture even to consider. From now on, memories of the way he'd once held her would have to suffice.

The storm finally wore itself out about an hour later and by nine was reduced to occasional gusts and the intermittent spatter of rain on the windows. Although the fire was still burning brightly, the tea she'd ordered had long since gone cold and Jenna was on the point of drawing a hot bath when another knock came at the door.

She opened it expecting to find someone from room service come to remove the tray, and instead came face-to-face with Edmund. Before she could draw breath, let alone speak, he stepped into the room, kicked the door closed behind him, swept her into his arms and kissed her full on the mouth.

When she most needed her wits about her, her mind simply took a leave of absence so that nothing stood between his seduction and her all too susceptible senses. She melted against him, helplessly enmeshed in pent-up longing.

The scent of him filled her, windswept cedar and salty sea air, and the faint residue of soap. The taste of him, coffee and peppermint, intoxicated her. Without let, her hand drifted over him, defining the texture of his heavy duffle jacket, his hair, the faint stubble of new beard on his cold cheek.

"So," he said, when at last he lifted his mouth from hers

and subjected her to a thorough inspection from his too-beautiful, too blue eyes, "you still want that divorce?"

Ignoring the question, she threw back one of her own. "How did you know where to find me?"

"I've known where you were every day for the last three weeks," he said, cupping her chin and studying her face as if he wanted to etch the memory of it in his mind forever. "Credit cards leave a trail of evidence behind them, my darling, and tracing a phone call takes mere seconds."

"But when I spoke to you earlier tonight, you were at home. How did you manage to get here so quickly?"

"Desperate situations call for desperate measures," he said, smoothing his hands over her hair. "Did you really think I was going to stand idly by and let you end our marriage without putting up a fight? I chartered a helicopter and I'd have been here a lot sooner if I hadn't been left cooling my heels while the weather calmed down."

"You should have saved yourself the trouble," she said, belated common sense reasserting itself. "Flying in at the last minute doesn't change a thing."

He smiled and she wished he'd been born with bad teeth, or better yet, had no teeth at all. A stone image would have found that smile hard to resist. "You look wonderful," he said, taking a step back the better to view her, and hooking one finger under the string of pearls around her neck. "That color suits you."

And she, fool that she was, blushed at the compliment and rejoiced that she hadn't changed since dinner. She knew that the dark green maternity dress, with its high empire waist and sweeping skirt, flattered her; that her slender, black pumps gave her added height and made her look less lumpily pregnant.

"Thank you," she said. "You look..." *Tall, dark and devastating. Handsome beyond imagining. Beloved!*

She stopped and bit her lip, hard. She needed to have her

mouth stapled shut! "Rather chilled," she said. "You shouldn't have risked pneumonia by coming here for nothing."

She might as well have been speaking in foreign tongues for all the attention he paid to what she said. "Our baby has grown," he remarked, his hand sliding intimately over her breasts to where junior was kicking away as if he knew it was his father's touch pressing lightly against him. "You're twice as big as you were the last time I held you."

She didn't want to be reminded of that last time. Nor was she about to permit a repeat performance, even though it was obvious that Edmund had decided to switch tactics and try to woo her with charm and seduction.

"You're wasting your time," she said, pushing him away. "I've made up my mind."

He strolled to the window and although he had his back to her, she knew he was watching her reflection in the dark glass. "And what would it take to change it, Jenna, my love?"

"Nothing," she said, sternly resisting the lure of *my love,* and *my darling,* and any other blandishment he might see fit to toss her way.

Lazily, he unbuttoned his jacket and removed it. "Don't you dare take off your clothes!" she said, in breathless panic.

He laughed, and it was as if summer breezed into the room, rich with warmth and sunlight. "The thought never crossed my mind."

"You're not staying, you know."

"I'll leave the minute you hear me out."

"Edmund," she said, a shade desperately, "we have nothing left to say to each other. I thought I made that clear already."

"I dropped the custody suit, Jenna."

"Dropped—?" Stunned, she stared at him, wishing he'd

turn around so that she could read the expression on his face. "When?"

"Shortly after you left, but not, I hasten to add, because you left. This isn't a ploy to win you back. I made my decision independently of anything to do with you and me."

"Then…why?" She was almost afraid to ask. Afraid that he was raising her hopes, only to dash them again and leave her more desolate than ever.

"I drove up to the Okanagan with every intention of bringing Molly back to town with me. When she saw me, she started to cry and begged her mother not to let me take her away. And Adrienne…" He heaved a sigh and slowly turned back to the room. No trace of his recent laughter remained. Instead, there was a soberness to the cast of his mouth, an introspective darkness in his eyes. "Adrienne told her not to be upset, that I was her daddy and would never hurt her, and she should go with me and have fun. But it wasn't enough. Molly still wouldn't look at me, let alone come to me. So Adrienne suggested I stick around for a while, have lunch with them, that sort of thing, to give her time to come around. And it shamed me. Because if the situation had been reversed, I'd have capitalized on it."

He cleared his throat and waited a second before continuing, "I stand just over six-two in my bare feet, Jenna, but at that moment I felt about two feet tall. My own daughter was afraid of me, my wife had left me because she, too, was afraid, and my ex-wife was showing a compassion and generosity I didn't deserve. What kind of jerk did that make me?"

She couldn't answer. He was as close to tears as she ever hoped to see him, and it was breaking her heart.

"I finally saw that you were right," he said, wrenching his emotions under control. "I'd lost sight of what mattered. The whole custody issue had taken on a life of its own that had nothing to do with Molly. I was blaming Adrienne and Bud when the person I should have blamed was myself.''

''No!'' she whispered, aghast. ''Whatever else you did wrong, you weren't responsible for Molly's accident, Edmund.''

''Indirectly, I'm afraid I was. I knew Bud was strapped for cash and that the machinery wasn't being properly maintained. That's probably why the brakes failed on the tractor, the day of the accident.''

''But you paid child support, didn't you?'' *Oh please,* she prayed, *tell me that you did!*

''I guess I deserve that question,'' he said. ''And yes, I did, every month without fail. But Bud wouldn't let Adrienne touch a cent of it. Every cheque I sent went straight into a trust account for Molly. Except for the gifts I gave her, everything she's owned since he married her mother came out of his pocket. He was scrupulous about being the provider. The way he saw it, he'd done more than take a wife, he'd taken on her child, as well. And that ate holes in me. I felt irrelevant. Instead of lending a hand with a few extra dollars when they were needed, I stood back and watched him struggle. That's why I have to take some responsibility for Molly's accident.''

''You're being too hard on yourself,'' she said. ''It was no one's fault.''

''Well, if it makes any difference, I've tried to put things right. I might be a real bozo at times, but I do learn, eventually. I've convinced Bud to let me help out with the cash flow. Things should be a bit easier for him from now on.''

He steepled his hands and pressed them to his mouth, then gave a shrug. ''And that's about it, Jenna. The next move's up to you. If you still want a divorce, I won't oppose it, nor will I use the baby as a bargaining tool. But,'' he said, moving with fluid grace to where she sat and falling to his knees at her feet, "if you'll give me another chance, I'll do my level best to prove myself worthy of it."

"Why? Because of the baby?"

"Because I love you," he said.

She turned her face aside and stared across the room, because looking at him and seeing the pain in his eyes was more than she could bear. "You make me afraid, Edmund," she said. "You touch my heart so easily; you always have. I've never been more vulnerable than I am with you."

He neither moved nor spoke. The only sound in the room was the shifting of a dying log in the hearth, the only motion that of sparks shooting up the chimney. For perhaps a full minute, he remained with one hand resting against her knee and his eyes tracking the expressions flitting across her face: hope warring with uncertainty; love fighting suspicion.

Finally, he rose to his feet and went to where he'd left his jacket. "I have done this to you," he said heavily. "My God, I should be shot."

He'd gone as far as the door before she found her voice and the courage to say what was in her heart. "Please don't go."

"Why not?"

She had never heard him sound so defeated. What had happened to her indomitable husband, the one whose favorite expression had once been *I won't allow...?*

"Because," she said, twisting in her seat to look at him, "every child deserves to grow up with both his parents there to tuck him in at night. And everyone deserves a second chance. Even us, Edmund."

He needed no further invitation. "I won't let you down again," he whispered hoarsely, drawing her into his arms and holding her as if he'd never let her go. "And if I ever get out of line again, do me a favor and give me a good swift kick in the rear."

"Oh, I can do better than that," she murmured, peeling

the duffle jacket off his shoulders and running her hands over the lovely firm planes of his chest. "Remember what I said before, about you keeping your clothes on?"

"Mmm-hmm." He nuzzled her neck.

"I've changed my mind," she said. "Will you please take them off?"

"I will," he said against her mouth. "Provided you do something for me."

She was ashamed of the little start of uneasiness to which that question gave rise. "And what's that?"

"Marry me," he said, undoing the buttons on the front of her dress and planting a kiss on her bare shoulder.

"We're already married."

"I know. But the last time, it was a furtive affair based on practical considerations." His mouth traveled to her ear, his voice lowered to a whisper. "This time, I'm asking you because I love you and I can't live without you. And I want the whole world to know it."

"But I'm pregnant," she objected. "Can't we wait until I've at least got a waist again?"

"Not a chance, sweet pea," he said, lifting her into his arms and making tracks for the bed. "I'm not risking losing you a second time."

It had taken them months to resolve their differences. It took only minutes for him to strip her naked, and only seconds longer for him to shed his own clothes. "I love you, Jenna Delaney," he said, just before he entered her.

Smooth and powerful, he filled her with his vibrant heat and she, as she always had, closed around him in a fusing of limbs and mouths; of hearts and minds and spirits. He was her soul mate. For the first time in weeks, perhaps for the first time ever, she felt truly complete.

"And I love you," she cried, clinging to him as the rhythm gained strength and the first spasms of slow sweet release took distant hold, rippling over her flesh, pebbling her skin, and turning her liquid with passion.

Outside, the wind picked up again, driving the waves relentlessly ashore. Inside the room, a different kind of passion ruled, no less implacable but infinitely more splendid.

EPILOGUE

THEY renewed their vows in November, on a day of crystal blue skies, and sunshine which still retained a faint breath of late summer.

The little church was full. Behind him on the left, his mother-in-law wore the look of a woman about to be martyred a second time. To the right, his mother adjusted her hat and whispered in his father's ear. Immediately behind them, Adrienne smiled encouragingly and Bud gave him the thumbs-up sign.

The air was heavy with the scent of flowers. The congregation hummed with anticipation. And he was nervous as a cat on hot bricks. What the devil had he been thinking, to suggest they go through with a second wedding when the first was still in effect? All this fuss, all these people...!

The organ droned to a halt, then struck up the opening notes of the familiar *Here Comes The Bride, Forty Inches Wide* wedding march. The door to the private room at the back of the church opened, and Molly came skipping out, angelic in white and dainty as a butterfly as she came down the aisle scattering rose petals. "Hi, Daddy," she piped, when she was still only halfway to the altar.

Even Valerie Sinclair cracked a smile.

Then Jenna appeared on her father's arm, and Edmund knew why he was there: so that he could keep the memory of how she looked alive in his heart long after they were both old and gray.

She wore blue, and carried a small bunch of creamy roses. Her long skirt brushed her ankles. The matching jacket hung full in front, proclaiming rather than trying to hide her pregnancy. Her eyes, her smile, her face…!

He swallowed and blinked. She was a vision! Once she'd looked at him as if he were her guardian angel, but he knew that, in fact, it was the other way around. She was the angel who'd brought him to the place he was now at: a man at peace and able to accept the compromises which were part and parcel of life.

"Jenna's got a baby in her tummy," Molly informed the congregation at large, as Jenna reached his side. "That's why it's sticking out."

A wave of laughter swelled from the pews.

He swallowed again, wiped his damp palms on the seat of his pants and wondered why such a woman would want to spend the rest of her life with a schmuck like him. He didn't deserve her. But, oh brother, did he need her! She was his lodestar, the one who kept him grounded. She had taught him what love was really all about.

"We are here today," the clergyman began, "to celebrate with Jenna and Edmund as they renew their marriage vows."

She'd pinned her hair up into some sort of fancy knot which she'd skewered in place with a couple of rosebuds. The diamond earrings which had been his wedding gift to her caught the light spearing through the mullioned windows and sparked with fiery brilliance.

"You're spoiling me," she'd said, when he'd presented them to her the night before.

"You're worth it," he'd replied.

Worth that, and a whole lot more! "An eternity ring," the jeweler had suggested, when, to mark their second wedding day, he'd asked to be shown something special to go with her existing engagement and wedding rings, but he'd not heard him right and thought the man said "maternity ring." Either way, the narrow gold band studded with diamonds and engraved with that day's date and the inscription *For Jenna: my wife, my love, my life.* did justice to only a fraction of what he felt in his heart.

"Edmund, do you take this woman—?"

"I do," he said, gripping her hands so tightly that she winced.

"Ahem!" the clergyman said. "—to be your wedded wife? Will you love her, honor her and keep her only unto you, so long as you both shall live?"

"And beyond," he said, winging it without warning. "For all eternity. I will cherish you forever, Jenna."

She turned a smile on him, so radiant that it put the sun to shame. Reflected in her lovely eyes he saw the affirmation of all that was in his heart and which, never in a million years, could he have put into words.

Eternity wasn't long enough for him to show her the depth of his love and commitment to her. But it would do for a start.

Harlequin invites you to experience the
charm and delight of

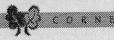

COOPERS CORNER

A brand-new continuity
starting in August 2002

HIS BROTHER'S BRIDE
by *USA Today* bestselling author
Tara Taylor Quinn

Check-in: TV reporter Laurel London and noted travel
writer William Byrd are guests at the new Twin Oaks
Bed and Breakfast in Cooper's Corner.

Checkout: William Byrd suddenly vanishes and while
investigating, Laurel finds herself face-to-face with
policeman Scott Hunter. Scott and Laurel face a painful past.
Can cop and reporter mend their heartbreak and get to the
bottom of William's mysterious disappearance?

HARLEQUIN®
Makes any time special ®

Visit us at www.cooperscorner.com

CC-CNM1R

The world's bestselling romance series.

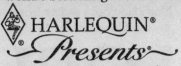

HARLEQUIN®
Presents~

Seduction and Passion Guaranteed!

A new trilogy by **Carole Mortimer**

BACHELOR COUSINS

Three cousins of Scottish descent—they're male, millionaires and marriageable!

Meet Logan, Fergus and Brice, three tall, dark, handsome men-about-town. They've made their millions in London, but their hearts belong to the heather-clad hills of their grandfather's Scottish estate.

Logan, Fergus and Brice are about to give up their keenly fought-for bachelor status for three wonderful women. Laugh, cry and read all about their trials and tribulations in their pursuit of love.

Look out for:
To Marry McCloud
On sale August, #2267

Coming next month:
To Marry McAllister
On sale September, #2273

Pick up a Harlequin Presents novel and you will enter a world of spine-tingling passion and provocative, tantalizing romance!

HARLEQUIN®
Makes any time special ®

Available wherever Harlequin books are sold.